I0712845

drawn to you

A HATE TO LOVE HOCKEY ROMANCE

MINNESOTA MAMMOTHS
BOOK 2

BRENDA ROTHERT

Copyright © 2024 by Brenda Rothert

All rights reserved.

No part of this book may be reproduced in any form or by any electronic or mechanical means, including information storage and retrieval systems, without written permission from the author, except for the use of brief quotations in a book review.

Cover design by Kari March

❀ Created with Vellum

one

JOSIE

I THOUGHT EATING PEANUT BUTTER AND JELLY sandwiches for lunch every day at work was the worst.

It's not.

Running out of jelly and bread before payday and eating a peanut butter sandwich made with the two heels of the bread loaf—that's actually the worst.

"That looks disgusting, Josie," my coworker Monica says as she unwraps the deli sandwich she had delivered from DoorDash.

"It's not bad," I lie, reaching for my water bottle to wash down the stale bread.

Monica is twenty-three and still lives at home. She doesn't know what it's like to be so broke you put five dollars' worth of gas at a time in your car because it's all you can afford.

I smile to myself because that's the one upside of my car getting repossessed last week: no more paying for gas. But now I have to pay for bus rides to work, which costs more than gas.

FML. I thought by age twenty-seven, I'd be a senior publicist at JG Publicity, getting my hair and nails done on my Friday lunch breaks to prepare for a weekend of barhopping in downtown Minneapolis.

Instead, I spent the first half of my lunch break listening to horrible on-hold music for the electric company before begging them to give me another week to pay my bill, leaving the rest of my break free for my dry sandwich and clueless coworker.

"Eww, I told them no tomato," she says, grimacing at her sandwich. "They mess my order up every time, I swear to God."

I lock eyes with Linda, one of the secretaries. She's a single mom of four who also has no tolerance for Monica's nonstop complaining.

"You want an apple?" Linda offers, taking one from her lunch bag.

"I'm good, thanks."

It's true what they say about people who have the least being the most generous. Linda knows I struggle, and she checks on me to make sure I'm okay.

I'm not okay, but I'm hanging in there. Making payments on a ten-thousand-dollar health insurance deductible for an unexpected gall bladder removal surgery eight months ago has put a major strain on my already meager finances. Those monthly five hundred- and fifty-dollar payments are the reason I'm waiting tables on weekends and clipping coupons.

Good thing I'm in line for a promotion. If I get it, the salary increase will change my life.

Convincing my boss to promote me, though? That's another story.

"Excellent font choices, Monica," Jane Garver says during our two p.m. group meeting. "The client wants to see a full presentation. I'll expect it to be ready by Monday afternoon."

"Absolutely," Monica says.

"Josie, did you steal that shirt from a homeless person?" Jane asks me, wrinkling her nose.

Or should I say, *Aunt* Jane. Having my aunt as a boss is worse than eating dry peanut butter sandwiches for every meal.

Monica cackles like the ass-kisser she is, and I smile tightly. My plain short-sleeved gray shirt may not have a designer label on it, but it's perfectly fine.

"I'm not seeing clients today, so I decided to dress down a bit."

Jane scoffs. "You'll need to go home and change before our four o'clock meeting."

"What meeting?"

She waves a hand. "I'll fill you in before. It's a job for a high-profile client, and you're perfect for it."

I straighten in my chair, taken aback. Perfect for it? Aunt Jane has never, since meeting me within a minute of my birth, thought I was perfect for anything.

"I'm sure you've all heard that Marnie is leaving us," Jane says crisply. "That creates an opening for a senior publicist. Junior publicists, show me your best work in the coming weeks and help make my decision easier."

Jane was so offended by Marnie's resignation that she told her not to even work out a two-week notice. She takes it personally when someone quits.

This job for a high-profile client is my chance to prove myself. I've worked here for five years, starting straight out of college as an intern. I like my job, and I want to stay here.

Publicists get to make people shine. Sometimes, we come in for damage control, helping clients rebuild their images. I like being part of a team that consists of me and my client.

I also like paying my electric bill on time and having a professional cut my hair instead of doing it myself.

Which means I have to get that promotion.

"Wait. What?" I gape at my boss a couple of hours later after finding out what my special assignment is.

"You'll be his...handler," Jane says brightly. "It couldn't be an easier job, really. You just watch over him and make sure he's not getting into trouble."

Arnold Morgan, owner of the Minnesota Mammoths pro hockey team, grins at Jane.

"I can't thank you enough for this, Jane. Bill me whatever rate you think is reasonable. And if she can keep him out of trouble for the whole three months, there'll be a considerable bonus."

"Bonus?" I turn to Arnold, distracted by his offer.

"Any bonus paid will go to the firm and it will be at my discretion what portion goes to you," Jane says.

I furrow my brow, mentally reviewing this assignment. Jane basically wants me to babysit a pro hockey player twenty-four seven. Stay with him and as Arnold said, "keep him out of trouble."

"Why?" I ask.

Jane's eyes flash with annoyance. "Because I own this firm, Josie, and--"

I cut in. "No, not that. Why does this guy need a handler? What kind of trouble has he gotten into?"

Arnold sighs through his nose. "Jane, is this conversation covered by our NDA?"

"Yes. Josie signed a blanket nondisclosure agreement and can't repeat anything from any client conversations."

Arnold nods and continues. "Dane has always liked the ladies. He recently slept with a woman who is legally separated from a well-known actor, and the actor has been tweeting about it. Dane would tell you he just likes to have a good time, but he's been dragged hungover from women's beds by teammates to catch the team bus more than once. He was arrested last week for public indecency after having sex with a woman on a park bench and then passing out. The woman stole all his clothes and his wallet afterward and when the sun rose, the police were called."

"What a headache for you, Arnold," Jane says, shaking her head. "Let us worry about this player so you can get back to the business of running your team."

Arnold exhales and smiles like he's just dumped the weight of the world from his shoulders.

"I appreciate it, Jane. You've come through for me every time I've hired you."

I want to ask what's happening here. Because they can't possibly expect *me* to do this job.

"How big is this guy Dane?" I ask.

"Dane Foster is six-three and a hundred and ninety pounds," Arnold says, reciting his roster stats.

I gesture at myself. "Five-four and a hundred

seventeen. How can I keep someone that size from doing anything?"

"Dane has been told this is his last shot," Arnold says. "If he steps out of line, you'll need to call his head coach immediately, and then this will all be over. No more PR nightmares; I don't care how great of a player he is." Arnold exhales hard. "But if you can keep him in line for the rest of the season--until the playoffs are over--that would be a great service to our team."

"Consider it done," Jane says, standing. "We won't take any more of your time, Arnold. I'll be in touch with the contract."

"I can give you a business credit card for all her expenses," he says, reaching for his wallet.

"No need. I'll bill your accounting people with receipts."

"Thanks, Jane." He glances at me. "And thanks to you too, Josie."

I smile weakly, not knowing what to say.

This assignment is bonkers. That's what I want to say, but I don't. And twenty-four seven? Who's going to take care of my cat, Mr. Darcy?

Jane walks Arnold out and then returns to her office, glaring at me.

"Where was your enthusiasm, Josie?"

My lips part and my eyes widen. "I don't see how I can do this. What this guy needs is more like a bodyguard."

"No, he needs someone who can remind him how important optics are. Which is literally your job."

I sigh softly.

"If you don't want this assignment, I'll give it to Monica."

And see that twit get promoted before me? Never. I need this promotion.

"I want it," I say. "I just want to succeed, and I'm not sure how."

"You're a bright girl. You'll figure it out."

A bright girl? I'll figure it out?

"But...where will I sleep?"

Jane sits down behind her desk, looks at her screen and starts typing. "I'm sure he has a couch, Josie."

"Do I get my own hotel room if I travel with him?"

She glares at me over the rim of her glasses. "Are you okay in the head? If you're asleep in a different room, how can you keep track of where he is?"

My aunt wants me to stay in a hotel room with

a six-three, one-hundred-ninety-pound man who "likes the ladies." Just great.

"Listen," she says, taking off her glasses and setting them on her desk. "I expect you to be within ten feet of this man at all times unless he's playing in a game, in which case I expect you to be watching that game. You will stick to him like a fly on glue. You will eat with him, you will travel with him, you will sleep in the same room as him. That's the assignment. And if you don't want it, I'll give it to someone who will jump at this opportunity."

"I want it."

She shakes her head, exasperated, and puts her glasses back on. "Get your things packed. You start tomorrow. You'll need to travel light."

I nod and stand up. "Okay. Thanks."

Deep down, I wonder if I'm getting this assignment because Jane believes in me or just because it sucks and she doesn't have the guts to ask another employee to give up their life for the next three months.

Either way, I'm going to succeed. I have to.

two

JOSIE

"Is this a joke?" Dane Foster looks between Arnold and his head coach, Tim Benton.

"Was your public indecency arrest a joke?" Tim fires back at him. "Because if that was all just a prank, we can clear this up real quick."

Dane hangs his head for a second. "Coach, I couldn't have known that woman would steal my clothes and handcuff me naked to a park bench."

I force myself not to smile. Arnold left out that detail yesterday in the meeting with me and Jane. Twenty-four hours have passed since then. I packed up some clothes and toiletries and now I'm in the head coach's office at the downtown Minneapolis arena where the Mammoths play.

"Funny thing, Dane," Tim says. "When you don't get so drunk you pass out, you can stop yourself from ending up in a situation like that."

Dane looks like a classic playboy. He's tall, lean and muscular, his dark hair cut short and his face coated with short, dark stubble. I can see how women fall fast for his perfect smile and bright-blue eyes, but I don't find him charming at all.

"I fucked up," Dane admits, casting a quick glance at me. "It won't happen again."

"You've fucked up a lot this season," Arnold says. "If you weren't such a great player, we'd have already dumped you off on another team. You're what team owners call a PR nightmare."

Arnold leans against the back wall of Tim's office, looking at his watch every thirty seconds or so. He doesn't seem to want to be here, and I don't, either. As someone who hates tension, I'd rather be literally anywhere.

"Thanks for that," Dane says wryly.

"Here's how this is going to work," Tim says. "No more women. No more drinking. No more bullshit. Josie will be like your shadow. She has my cell number, and if you break any of these rules, she will immediately call me. This is your last shot."

"No." Dane crosses his arms and looks directly at his coach. "This is over the line. No one else on this team has some college intern following them around."

I won't let that slide.

"I'm twenty-seven and I'm a publicist at JG Publicity," I say, somehow managing to keep my voice level and confident.

He gives me a dismissive glance. "I don't care who you are. No one's going to follow me around and tell me what I can and can't do."

Arnold scoffs with disgust. "Tim, I told you this was a waste of time. I've had it with his attitude."

Dane responds before his coach has a chance to. "You can't control me every second of the day, Arnold. You don't own me just because you signed me to a contract. And speaking of my contract, I'm sure my agent will have a few things to say about this."

"You're a petulant child," Arnold yells. "I'm done with you."

"Gentlemen," Tim says, putting his palms out

in an effort to calm them. "Let's all take a step back."

The room goes silent for a few seconds, but Dane and Arnold still look like they want to step outside and fistfight.

"Dane, you're my top player, but your personal life is out of control," Tim says. "And you know how bad it is for our team's image. Your teammates deserve better."

The fight falls from Dane's expression. After a moment, he nods.

"I'm sorry, Coach."

"This has been run past our legal team, and it's not a violation of your contract terms," Tim says. "If you do what you're supposed to do and stay out of trouble, you won't even know Josie's there."

Dane sits up straight in his chair, his expression a mix of aggravation and resignation. "Is she moving into my house?"

I wish they would have had this conversation without me here. Dane asked the question like I'm soap scum or a leaky pipe--an annoyance no one wants around.

"Yes," Tim says. "And traveling with the team. We'll call her your assistant if anyone outside the organization asks about her."

Dane sneers. "That makes me seem high maintenance."

Arnold bursts out laughing in a hearty, genuinely amused laugh. "It's a little late to start caring about your reputation."

Dane turns to look at me. It's the first time he's given me anything more than a quick glance. I can feel him sizing me up based on my clothes, my hair, my expression. And I don't like it.

"What about the cat?" he asks.

Mr. Darcy, the black cat I adopted from an animal shelter last year, meows from his spot in my arms like he knows he's being discussed.

"He's with me," I say.

Scoffing, Dane glares at his coach. "I hate cats."

"My heart bleeds for you," Arnold says flatly.

"The cat's not coming," Dane says. "She can follow me around, but she's not moving a cat into my house."

Tim gives me an apologetic look. "Is there anywhere else you can leave the cat?"

The only person I'd trust to care for Mr. Darcy is my best friend, Lina, and she's allergic to cats.

"No. But he's not much trouble."

"He can't come on road trips," Tim says.

"I understand."

Dane sighs dramatically. I don't like him. I can't wait to get under his skin by asking how it felt to wake up naked and handcuffed to a park bench. If he's not going to make this easy for me, I won't make it easy for him, either.

"I think we're done here," Arnold says, pushing away from the wall.

"Wait," Dane says. "How long will she be following me around?"

"For the next three months or until you screw up next," Arnold says, narrowing his eyes at Dane. "Guess which one my money's on?"

Dane starts to say something but stops himself.

"Well, look at that," Arnold says. "He does have some restraint. It's just buried deep down in there. Probably hangs out with his conscience."

Dane scratches his head, and I think I'm the only one who notices he's doing it with his middle finger. Cheeky.

Arnold gives me a paternal look and puts a hand on my shoulder. "Josie, if you have any problems or need any expenses covered, you call me. Or Tim, if you're on the road."

"Th--" I start to speak, but my voice is strangled, so I clear my throat. "Thank you."

I sound timid, but I'm not. At the moment, though, I want to crawl under Tim's massive wood desk and never come out. But I remind myself I'm a professional, here to do a job.

Three months. If I can do this, I'll get the promotion. I'll be able to afford something other than spaghetti and pancakes for dinner.

Takeout. How I miss takeout. Just the thought of those heavenly-smelling little white boxes from Hot Wok sends a pang to my stomach.

I'll be able to save money again. Buy new shoes. I need this to work.

Dane stands up, and I follow suit. He looks at me like I'm a muddy stray dog he just found. I force my chin to remain level.

I won't let him know how intimidated I am.

"Let's go, I guess," he says with absolutely no enthusiasm.

I move to pick up my fully stuffed backpack, and he grabs it by the handle at the same time.

"You don't have to carry it," I say, even though it weighs at least thirty pounds and my back still hurts from carrying it here.

"I've got it," he says gruffly, not even looking at me. "Where's your other stuff?"

"This is all I could carry, so it's all I brought."

"Which lot are you parked in?"

"I don't have a car."

His eyes flash with annoyance. "Awesome. Guess you're riding with me."

"Apologies for the imposition," I say sarcastically. "I know how massively difficult it is to have someone sitting in your passenger seat."

He ignores me and hikes the backpack over his shoulder.

"What'd you put in this thing, bricks?" he grumbles.

"Nope." I give him a big smile. "It's the body of the last guy who pissed me off."

He shakes his head. "So you're a comedian, too."

"When you work in publicity, you have to have a sense of humor."

He leads the way down a concrete-floored hallway in the basement level of the arena. Now that he can't see me looking, I let my gaze wander. The definition in his shoulder and arm muscles shows through the lightweight long-sleeved gray shirt he's wearing.

This guy is a walking cliché. All he needs is a blond trophy wife with an aesthetically pleasing IG account of couple's photos hashtagged #myperson and #myworld.

It's only three months. Fewer if they don't make the playoffs. I can put up with anything as long as it has an end date.

I follow him onto an elevator, where he scans a badge and presses a button. When we step out, we're in a small, nearly empty underground parking deck.

"This is me," he says, pushing a button on a key fob to unlock a black Range Rover. "Don't let the cat run loose in my car, I don't want hair all over it."

So charming. I force myself to stay quiet because, technically, he is a JG client. Whether I like him or not, I have a job to do.

As soon as we're both in the car with our seat belts buckled, he checks the rearview mirror, backs out of his parking place and gives me a pointed look.

"If that thing pisses on my furniture, it's going to the shelter."

I narrow my eyes at him. "Touch my cat and I'll stab you in your sleep, asshole."

"Christ," he mutters. "This is going to be the longest three months of my life."

"Let's both hope your team chokes and you don't make the playoffs."

He scoffs and tightens his one-handed grip on the steering wheel but says nothing.

Smart. The less Dane Foster and I talk to each other, the better off we'll both be.

three

JOSIE

We ride in silence until Dane stops at the gated entrance to a modern limestone building with landscaping that looks straight out of a gardening magazine. He turns to speak to me as the gate goes up after scanning a sticker on his lower windshield.

"Don't share my address or any details about me with anyone," he warns. "Don't take any photos inside my home. My privacy is important to me."

I smile to myself, thinking about all the photos people may have taken of him handcuffed to that park bench. God willing.

"Our agency has higher-profile clients than

you," I say lightly, though in reality, the Mammoths are top tier. "My job is to help ensure your privacy, not violate it."

"Keep it that way. I don't let many people inside my home."

The building is located just outside the city, the long driveway leading to an underground garage. The lighted garage has four wide doors, one of which Dane opens by pressing a button near his rearview mirror.

The garage is big enough for two cars, and a dark-gray Jeep Wrangler is parked inside. Dane pulls up next to it, parks and exits his car, grabbing my bag from the back seat.

I hold Mr. Darcy close, concerned he might jump out of my arms and hide. We take a small door out of the garage and Dane pushes some buttons on a keypad, closing the garage and locking the door.

An elevator takes us up to a tiled foyer with four doors, modern art displayed on the walls. Dane enters a code into a keypad and opens the door, stepping aside so I can enter first.

Now he wants to be a gentleman? It's a little late for that. I walk into the apartment, which is bright and open. The windows run from floor to ceiling, some of them extra wide to maximize the view of the Minneapolis skyline.

I've never been inside such a luxurious home. The floors are grayish-brown wood, the furniture all neutral brown and cream shades. The kitchen has white cabinets, marble counters and a huge island with six barstools.

"The guest room is this way," Dane says, leading me down a hallway.

Just like the rest of the house, the guest room looks like no one lives in it. A white down comforter covers the queen-size bed, not a wrinkle in sight. There's a small wood chest of drawers and a walk-in closet.

"I'll keep the litter box in here," I say.

He cringes. "Fine."

Then he sets my bag on the bed and leaves the room. I stare at the open doorway for a few seconds, unsure what to do.

What if he leaves? Should I ask him if he plans to leave?

I can't close the door to the room to keep Mr. Darcy inside because then I won't be able to hear the door if Dane leaves. My cat is very attached to me, though, so I doubt he'll go anywhere.

I set Mr. Darcy on the furry throw folded at the

foot of the bed. He stretches out and curls up on the throw, freeing up my hands.

First things first, I get on the Instacart app and order a litter box, cat litter, iced tea, and a few other groceries. Jane shocked me by depositing an extra five hundred dollars into my bank account for expenses, so I'm not completely broke for once.

I unpack my clothes, put my bag in the closet and pick up one of the paperbacks I unpacked.

Sighing softly, I sit down on the bed. I already miss my shabby little apartment. The bathroom faucet leaks and it's drafty when it's cold outside, but it's filled with books, plants and comfy, well-worn furniture. It doesn't feel sanitized and vacant like this place.

I'm stuck here, though. At least for now. Might as well make the best of it. I pick up Mr. Darcy, who meows in protest and carry him to the living room, where I sit down in a chair and start reading my book.

Dane walks into the living room and puts his hands on his hips, his expression annoyed.

"I'm going to a birthday party for a teammate tonight at a restaurant downtown," he says.

"What time?"

"Leaving at five thirty."

I panic inside, wishing I'd brought some nice dresses. I packed a capped-sleeve black pantsuit and black ballet flats that will have to do.

"Am I allowed to ride with you, or should I take an Uber?" I ask.

He scowls. "You can ride with me, but you don't need to be beside me all night. People will think we're together."

Please. Anyone who heard me use words with multiple syllables would know I wasn't with Dane. A woman would need below-average intelligence to put up with his shit.

"I doubt that," I say sweetly. "But don't worry, I'll sit at the bar by myself like the sad little troll I am."

"I'm not waiting if you aren't ready to go at five thirty," he says.

"I'll be ready."

With a nod, he turns and walks into the kitchen.

"What the fuck?" he says a few seconds later, his voice louder than necessary. "Get your ass down!"

My head whips sideways to check the spot next to me on the couch where Mr. Darcy was sitting just a minute ago. He's gone.

"Your asshole cat is on my kitchen counter," Dane practically growls at me.

I run into the kitchen to corral Mr. Darcy.

"Get down!" I tell him.

He ignores me, so I walk over and sweep him off the counter.

"Where's that thing going to piss?" Dane demands.

I glare at him. "He's not a thing; he's a cat, and I ordered him a litter box on Instacart. It'll be here within an hour."

"I don't want him on the kitchen counters."

"Relax," I say, walking into the living room to pick up my book. "I'll take him to the bedroom. Go look in the mirror and kiss your muscles, or whatever it is you do to chill out."

I walk back into the guest room, close the door and set Mr. Darcy down.

Tonight I'll get to find out if Dane is an asshole all the time or just to me.

AT 5:29 P.M. SHARP, I WALK OUT OF THE BATHROOM across from the guest room. Dane is standing at the front door, his gaze making a quick up-and-down sweep of me.

This outfit looks great on me. My cleavage is on

point and my waist looks smaller than it is. I showered and blew out my long, dark hair, taming the natural waves. With some light makeup, I'm presentable for pretty much any restaurant bar.

"You ready?" Dane asks.

I nod, and he once again holds the door for me. Which is kind of hilarious, really. Why hold the door for a woman you treat with contempt?

One thing I'll give Dane--he cleans up well. He's wearing gray dress pants and a white dress shirt with the sleeves rolled up. He's clean-shaven and smells like expensive cologne.

We take the elevator down to the garage in silence, and once we're inside the Range Rover, I try to break the ice.

"So, which of your teammates is having a birthday party?"

"Archer Holt."

He pulls out of the garage, the gate at the end of the driveway opening more quickly this time.

"Look, I know you don't want me to be here," I say. "But I'm only here because my boss assigned me to be. Both of us were put in this situation by our bosses."

"I know that." His gaze remains fixed on the road.

"It'll be a lot easier if we can get along."

"I'm trying, but I'm not used to having anyone in my space."

He's trying? This is him *trying*?

"Is there anything I can do to make it easier?" I ask.

"Don't talk so much."

My lips part with shock. Does he treat everyone this way?

"You know, I'm not even a little surprised some woman stole your wallet and handcuffed you to a park bench," I snap. "Good for her. She did a solid for womankind."

"Great, a thief just moved in with me," he grumbles.

"Oh, shove it, asshat. You don't have anything worth stealing. Keep your matching Crate and Barrel dishes and boring brown furniture."

He pushes a button on the steering wheel and turns on music. It's Eminem, and he turns up the volume. Obviously, he feels called out about his stock photo apartment and can't think of a response.

We spend the rest of the drive to the restaurant with the music loud, and when he parks the car and turns it off, he immediately gets out and heads for the restaurant entrance, not bothering to see if I'm following.

For a moment, I consider telling Jane to give this job to Monica. Three months of this, twenty-four seven, is too much.

My stubbornness won't allow it, though. I tuck my paperback, wallet and phone against my waist and walk inside the restaurant.

four

JOSIE

When I step inside the upscale steak house, I'm
surprised to find Dane waiting for me.

"Look, you don't need to sit at the bar," he says.
"Just don't hang on me and make us look like a
couple."

His efforts to be nice fall short, to say the least. I
could nod to keep the peace, but that's just not me.

"I don't want to touch you," I say in my most
professional tone. "Not even a little bit. Believe me
when I tell you my actions will *never* make people
think I'm with you or trying to get with you."

"What, like I'm so awful?" He lowers his brows, offended.

Yes. Yes, he is. But I'm saved from answering that impossible question when someone comes up from behind Dane and puts an arm around his shoulders.

"Hey, now we can start the party!" he says, grinning widely.

Dane's friend sees me and offers a hand.

"Hi, I'm Aaron Parker."

"Parker, this is Nosy," Dane says. "Arnold hired her to babysit me for the rest of the season."

I shoot Dane a glare and then shake Aaron's hand. "I'm Josie, nice to meet you."

Aaron shakes my hand, still smiling. He has warm eyes and seems friendly.

"Likewise, Josie. And good luck keeping this one in line. Once he gets a few drinks in him, he turns into a werewolf." He claps Dane on the back. "Should we go join the party?"

My heart races nervously as I follow the men to a back room of the steak house. I've never felt so out of place. When I work for top-tier clients, I'm part of a team and we're talking public relations.

Here, I don't know anyone except Dane who would rather hang out with anyone but me. I fight my urge to slip off to the bar and read my book because I can't keep an eye on him from there.

There are around twenty-five people in the room, some standing and talking with drinks in hand and others seated at the long table set for around forty people.

I make eye contact with a woman talking to two other women, and she smiles, so I walk over.

"Hi, I'm Josie Garver."

"Hey Josie, I'm Jenn Rogers, Aiden's wife. This is my sister Carrie and this is Elena Parker, Aaron Parker's wife."

"Nice to meet you guys."

They're all beautiful. Jenn and Carrie both have long blond hair, blue eyes and are tall and lean. Elena is biracial, her eyes a beautiful coffee brown and her hair a mass of thick, tightly coiled black curls that look like they belong in a hair product commercial.

"Did you come with Dane?" Jenn asks.

I have to be quick on my feet to answer the question diplomatically.

"I did, but in a strictly professional capacity. I just started working for the team."

Jenn's expression brightens. "Oh! Welcome to the family. Are you a trainer?"

"No, I work in public relations. I'm more of an assistant to Dane."

Elena bursts out laughing. "Say no more, sis. That one needs all the help he can get."

I scoff softly and smile, grateful to have met women who know Dane. "Is he always so...abrasive?"

"Dane?" Jenn furrows her brow, confused. "He's a total sweetheart."

"He can be very charming," Elena says. "But only on his terms. He never takes women to his home. My friend Tara went out with him a couple of times. It was dinner followed by sex at her place both times. When she asked if he'd go out with some of her friends or if they could make dinner at his place, he ghosted her."

"Sounds like an asshole," Carrie said.

I want to vent to these women like friends, but I can't. This is a situation where I can gather information from them, but professionally, I can't share anything with them they don't already know.

Elena grabs a drink from the tray of a passing server and passes it to me. "Girl, you probably need this."

I take a sip of what I think is peach champagne, though I'll only be able to drink a little bit of it.

When I sneak a glance at Dane, he's got a bottled beer in hand and is having an animated conversation with Aaron and another man.

Already breaking his coach's no-alcohol rule. Awesome. I don't want to be forced to drive us home in his hundred-thousand-dollar car because he gets wasted.

Within a few minutes, a lovely woman in a well-cut black dress stands at the head of the table and asks everyone to sit down. A man in a gray suit with a blue dress shirt and no tie walks over to her, slides his arm around her waist and kisses her.

I look around, thinking this would be a good time for me to slip off to the bar. They surely didn't plan on having a seat for me, and I don't want to blow a big chunk of the money Jane gave me on dinner here.

Dane approaches me and my heart skips a beat as I get my first look at him not scowling or sneering. He's half smiling and I realize he's very good-looking.

I lean closer to him, getting a nice smell of his cologne. "I'll be at the bar."

"Just sit down," he says, pulling out a chair for me.

Not wanting to make a scene, I sit, and he sits in

the seat next to mine. Servers fill water glasses as the woman at the head of the table smiles at the group gathered.

"For anyone who doesn't know me, I'm Lauren Holt," she said. "We so appreciate everyone taking the time to be here with us tonight to celebrate my husband's birthday. It's an extra special one this year because it's the last time we'll be a family of two on his birthday."

She's glowing as she reaches down to the table and lifts up a little white onesie with black writing that says, "Baby Holt due 9.3.23."

The table erupts into cheers and applause, Archer and Lauren both looking overjoyed. I feel like I don't belong in this intimate moment between them and their Mammoths team family. It's clear the men on this team and their partners care a great deal for each other.

A lean man with short, dark hair stands up and motions over a server.

"We'll need a few bottles of your best champagne," he says.

The server nods and says, "Right away, sir. We have a very nice Krug."

"Dane, who's your friend?" a man asks from the other side of the table.

Dane doesn't even look at me as he answers. "This is Josie; she's my bodyguard. She prefers to be called Nosy."

I shake my head.

The man who ordered the champagne leans forward in his seat and looks down the table at us.

"Arnold hired her to keep Dane on the rails."

There are scoffs and laughs around the table, a few people muttering, "Good luck." I look at Dane and his annoyed expression is back.

"Do you not think you're a pain in the ass?" I ask him before I even have time to think about it.

Laughter breaks out around us and one guy says, "I like her."

Dane gives me a wry look. "I think I can be too much fun for some people."

The champagne-ordering man howls. "Was it fun spreading your cheeks to get searched when they booked you into jail in Chicago?"

Dane shoots him a glare. "If you'd answered the phone, that wouldn't have happened."

"I bailed you out before the bus left," he says with a shrug.

"Didn't they pull a machete and a full-size turkey out of your anal cavity?" someone quips.

"And a velvet painting of Elvis," another teammate says.

"Damn, dude. That thing must be *stretched*."

"Enough, assholes," Dane says with a scowl. "Tonight is about Archer and Lauren."

The laughter dies down as several servers come into the room with bottles of champagne on ice. More servers follow with bread and salads for everyone, and I pull off a bite of a slice of bread immediately, because I'm feeling lightheaded from not eating since breakfast.

I pass on the offer of champagne because I can't stand the thought of only drinking a few sips of something so expensive. For the toast to Archer and Lauren's good news, I use my glass of water.

Dane, on the other hand, downs a full glass of champagne, refills it and orders another beer.

I lean over to speak softly in his ear. "You're not driving home."

"Okay, Mom."

"I'm serious," I whisper.

"Fine."

We spend the next couple of hours eating a delicious meal of steak, au gratin potatoes, several kinds of vegetables and chocolate lava cake. Elena switches chairs with the person on the other side of me halfway through so I have someone to talk to. She makes me laugh and actually enjoy myself, even with Dane on my other side.

The man who ordered the champagne for everyone is the Mammoths' team captain, Dalton Lorenzo, and he picks up the tab at the end of the night, not even blinking as he fills out the receipt. This is his first year as team captain after the team's longtime captain retired.

"Do you think Aaron can help me get him to the car?" I ask Elena softly because Dane has had a lot to drink and if he falls over in the parking lot, I won't be able to get him up.

"Of course."

"I'm fine, Nosy," Dane says, aggravated. "Just drive us home so we can see how much of my house your cat has destroyed."

Dalton laughs from nearby. "You have to live with that bastard?"

I shrug. "For the time being."

"Go with God," he says, still grinning.

Dane is right--he's fine to walk to the car, and he does. Once we're on the road, he turns to me.

"That wasn't so bad, was it?"

"It was fun. Everyone on your team seems really nice. Other than you, I mean."

He laughs and balls his coat up against the car window, resting his head. "You just don't know me, Nosy. I can be the nicest guy there is."

I seriously doubt that. But I'm too tired to argue anymore. Tomorrow afternoon, we're leaving for a road trip with the team.

That'll be the real test. Dane's worst behavior seems to happen on road trips. I'm going to need a good night of sleep to prepare myself.

And also a whole lot of luck.

five

JOSIE

THE MINNESOTA MAMMOTHS' PLANE IS PAINTED IN the team's purple and teal colors and the logo-- not surprisingly, a mammoth--is painted on the tail. We boarded directly from the tarmac after bypassing the usual airport security and doing a quick, private screening.

The plane's exterior is impressive, but it's got nothing on the interior. Legroom? Several feet for every passenger. Leather? Covering every extra-large seat. There are a couple of built-in tables with four seats each, and those were the first ones players took, a card game already in progress at one. A flight attendant in a purple uniform passes out bottled Fiji water.

When we got home last night, Dane went straight to bed. Today, we've hardly spoken. He showed me how to use his washing machine and I mentioned on the drive here that I would probably get sick on the flight. That was it.

"Excuse me," Dane says to the flight attendant, whose nametag identifies her as Janet.

"Yes, Mr. Foster?"

"Can my bodyguard get some barf bags? She gets sick on planes."

Janet gives me a confused look, probably over the bodyguard thing, and then smiles brightly at Dane. "Of course. We also have Dramamine if that might help."

"You don't by any chance have any tranquilizers, do you?" I ask, half joking.

More like thirty percent joking. I hate flying more than just about anything. I hardly slept last night because I kept envisioning dying in a fiery plane crash over this stupid assignment I should have let Monica have.

Janet gives me a sympathetic look. "I'd bring you a drink, but you shouldn't have alcohol with motion sickness medication. Let me grab that so we can get it in you before takeoff."

"Thank you."

Dane slides into a window seat, and I take the seat next to him, clutching my backpack to my chest and resting my head against the seat back, my eyes squeezed shut.

"I take it you don't fly much?" Dane asks, amused.

"I've flown twice and it was awful both times."

"How old were you?"

"Twelve the first time, twenty the second time."

I swore after the second flight from Minneapolis to Washington, DC, for a class in college that I'd never set foot on a plane again. We hit major turbulence and I was so sick on the flight there that I called my dad and he rented a car for me to drive home.

And now, here I am, not just on an airplane, but on an airplane next to Dane.

"I really like this suit; don't puke on it," he says, void of empathy.

I can't even focus on sparring with him right now. It's all I can do to breathe in and out.

"Here you go, hon," Janet says from beside me. "I brought you water and apple juice because sometimes juice helps when people are feeling nauseous."

She passes me the drinks, a packet of Dramamine and several large white bags.

Even the barf bags are better than the ones on commercial airplanes. I thank Janet and open the bottle of water. Dane tugs on my backpack.

"Stop," I tell him, holding on to it.

His trademark glare appears. "It has to go under the seat. Let go."

Reluctantly, I release my hold on the only security blanket I have. A memory pops into my head uninvited: on the flight to DC in college, I sat next to Jack Smallwood, a guy I was interested in. He was interested back until I threw up my bacon-and-egg breakfast in his lap.

The absolute mortification I felt hits me all over again. A flight attendant moved me to another seat so they could clean Jack up, and through my continuous vomiting, I could hear Jack's disgusted comments about bacon chunks.

"Take the medicine, Nosy," Dane urges impatiently. "We're taking off soon."

I'm dizzy. My heart is racing. I don't want to endure the humiliation of puking in front of an entire professional hockey team.

"Why is it so hot in here?" I ask weakly.

Dane takes the packet of pills from my hand, tears it open and dumps the pills out.

"Take them," he orders.

I take the pills, put them in my mouth and chase them with a sip of water, my stomach churning. My hairline is wet with sweat and I don't even want to think about how pathetic I must look.

Someone cheers loudly from the table where the card game is being played.

"Pay up!" a male voice yells.

"You're the luckiest son of a bitch I've ever known," someone grumbles.

I lift my head from the back of the seat and a powerful wave of nausea hits. We haven't even taken off yet, and I'm already sick. Frantically, I open a bag and bring it up to my mouth just in time to hurl into it.

"That's helpful," Dane grumbles. "You just puked up the medicine."

Like I did it on purpose or something. I want to punch him. Right in his smug face.

"Can you not?" I snap as Janet crouches beside me.

"What can I do for you?" she asks, passing me a wet washcloth.

I smile weakly as I take the washcloth and clean my mouth. "I don't know. I'm hot and dizzy."

"How about a little battery-operated fan and a clean, wet washcloth for the back of your neck?"

I nod gratefully. "Thank you."

"I'm guessing you've had a bad experience with flying?"

"Yes. Really bad."

She takes the bag I just used, folding it closed and sealing it. "It's nerves. I see it all the time. People who have gotten sick are so convinced it'll happen again that they make themselves sick before we even take off."

Dane interjects himself into our conversation. "So you're saying it's all in her head?"

I reach for my seat belt and unfasten it. "I'm not sitting here."

"I'm sorry, we're too close to takeoff for you to move," Janet says as the pilot makes an announcement. "I need you to put it back on. As soon as we're in the air, I can bring you that fan."

Reluctantly, I refasten my seat belt, leaning my head against the seat back and closing my eyes.

"How much are you getting paid for this?" Dane asks me.

"Not enough."

The plane is rolling now, everyone around me carrying on conversations like everything is fine. I squeeze the armrests, telling myself to relax. Flights take off and land safely all the time. It's supposed to be safer than driving a car.

I am a professional. I can do this.

"Go to your happy place," Dane says dismissively. "Like a library. You always have a book with you; you must like libraries."

My stomach lurches as the captain slows and announces we're about to take off. Eyes still closed, I open another bag so it's ready when I need it.

"Don't puke again," Dane says. "Come on, Nosy, where's your happy place? Let's talk it out."

"She sick?" someone asks from nearby.

"Yep," Dane answers.

He returns his attention to me. "Where's the happy place? Is it a beach?"

He has no concern at all for my well-being. He just doesn't want me puking next to him. The plane starts moving again and I take a deep breath in and out.

"It's hot," I say, my hands aching from squeezing the armrests so hard.

"Stop thinking about that," he says, annoyed. "Happy place. Lapping waves. Frozen drinks."

The plane is moving faster now and my stomach is in a free fall.

"That is my happy place," I say, cringing. "It's filled with flames. It's a literal inferno." I press myself against the back of the seat as the plane lifts off. "The guys who invented pantyhose and shapewear are there and it's run by a guy named Lucifer."

"Your happy place is hell?" he asks, confused.

"As long as you're not there, yes," I manage, bringing the bag up to my mouth.

"Real nice, Nosy," he grumbles. "I'm trying to help you here and that's the thanks I get?"

I can't hold on any longer. It's a good thing I didn't eat this morning because my stomach won't rest until it's empty. I puke into the bag, tears running from the corners of my eyes.

"Poor thing," someone says from behind us. "My son gets motion sickness."

I turn away from Dane, keeping a tight hold on the bag. We're flying from Minneapolis to Tampa, so I may be in for three hours of this.

And it's just the beginning of this road trip. From Tampa, we're flying to Boston, then to Toronto and then home.

I feel the heat of Dane's body as he leans closer

to me. "I'm putting my headphones on. Will you nudge me before you barf so I can try to move out of the way?"

He's the most inconsiderate jackass I've ever had the misfortune of working for. He deserves to be puked on.

"Yeah, I'll nudge you with my foot," I fire back. "It might hurt."

He chuckles. "With your little pixie feet? I doubt it."

Somehow, I have to get my hands on one of those park bench photos. I'd never share them with anyone, but to get to see Dane in a compromising position?

That, I would enjoy a lot.

six

JOSIE

"Josie, wake up!"

With a gasp, I open my eyes and survey the scene around me. I'm sitting at a long table in a bar, the rest of the table filled with Mammoths players passing around shot glasses filled with amber liquid.

"You want one?" Dalton Lorenzo asks me, holding out a shot glass.

I recognize his voice as the one who woke me up. I can't believe I fell asleep in a crowded bar.

Then again, I'm about to doze off again. After hardly sleeping last night and being sick for the whole three-hour flight to Tampa, I wandered off the plane in a daze.

The weather is nice here. It's in the '70s. Normally, I'd love to check out the local scenery. But after a two-hour dinner with the team at an Italian restaurant, I was ready for bed. Unfortunately, though, Dane wanted to go out with his teammates. So here I am, technically on the job but also unable to stay awake.

"No, thanks," I tell Dalton, looking around the table for Dane.

He was right next to me, but now there's another player sitting there. I think his name is Banks.

Banks gives me a tight grin and says, "Hey, you've got a little…"

He wipes his chin and I do the same. *Hell.* I was drooling. In front of the same people who saw me puke so many times I lost count. This day just keeps on giving.

"Where's Dane?" I ask after scanning every face at the table.

Banks gestures behind him. "Follow the scent of cheap perfume."

I jump out of my seat and start the search,

quickly finding him standing at a tall round table with a redhead who's gazing adoringly at him.

"I play for them," he says earnestly. "Those orphans, they're..." He looks away, pretending he can't continue because he's so choked up. "It's not about me anymore. I'm sure you can imagine how hard life is at an orphanage in Siberia, and I give anonymously because I don't want any credit. The credit goes to them for"

I can't take any more of his bullshit. I approach the table and swipe the half-empty beer bottle.

"You heard the rules as clearly as I did. No alcohol and no women."

He shakes his head and locks eyes with the redhead. "Cassie, this is one of our team interns. She's got some issues."

I open the camera on my phone, seething. "I've got issues? You're the one who's gonna have issues when I send this photo to Tim."

He narrows his eyes and says, "Fine. I'll send your boss this one."

He pushes a couple of buttons on his phone screen and flips it to face me. There's a photo of me sitting at the table I just got up from, my head bowed and my mouth open as I sleep.

"You asshole. You know how sick I was on the plane, but I still have to follow you around and I'm doing my best."

"Get back to your nap," he says. "I'm just talking here; it's not a big deal."

I pass the bottled beer to a passing server and say, "Can you throw this away, please?"

"Sure."

"That's not very nice," Cassie says to me like I'm a little kid who won't share my toy.

I stare at her for a second, too shocked to speak. Her shirt is cut so low her nips are almost showing and she was buying every word of Dane's story about helping orphans. Her insight into this situation is definitely not needed.

"It's not very nice?" I finally manage. "I'm being paid to watch over him and make sure he stays out of trouble."

She lights up. "Oh, that sounds like a fun job! I could do that!"

Dane grins at her. "I'm sure you'd be great at it."

I roll my eyes, fed up with his games.

"We're going back to the hotel," I say.

"Can I come too?" Cassie asks Dane.

"No," I answer for him.

Dane and I have a double queen room. It's bad enough I have to stay in the same room as him, there's no way anyone else is coming in.

For a few long seconds, Dane and I engage in a stare-off. I'm so tired my eyes hurt, but I refuse to look away. I won't lose out on my promotion because he can't keep his dick in his pants for two to three months.

Finally, he gives.

"I guess I need to get going," he says. "It was great meeting you, Cassie."

"Oh." Her happy expression slides away. "Okay."

It's almost eleven p.m., and if I don't get to bed soon, I'm going to fall asleep standing up. We walk back to the table, where a few of the seats are empty from people leaving.

"You need to be more subtle next time," Dane says in a low tone, sounding irritated. "And don't tell anyone you're getting paid to make sure I stay out of trouble."

That was a misstep on my part. But him telling me to be more subtle? That's laughable.

"You want me to be subtle when you're lying your ass off to unsuspecting women in hopes of spending a few hours in bed with them and never calling again?"

He presses his lips into a thin line, the muscle in his jaw flexing.

"We're taking off," he announces to the table. "Anyone want to ride with us?"

Banks and another player ride in our Uber, which ends up being a minivan. When we get into our hotel room, Dane turns on the lights and immediately pulls his shirt off over his head. I can't help letting my gaze linger on him for a few seconds. His torso is so cut with defined muscles that he looks Photoshopped. His chest hair is dark. I force myself to look away.

Dane is sifting through an overnight bag when I steal another glance, this time taking in his broad shoulders. I can see how seducing women is so easy for him--he has the looks to back up his game.

"You want me to autograph a poster for you or something?" he asks.

"What?" I look away, embarrassed he caught me staring.

"So you've got something to admire when I'm sleeping or whatever." He grins, clearly enjoying this. "I've got an online fan club; I could send you the link to join."

"Go fuck yourself. I was looking out of curiosity, not admiration."

He laughs. "Well, I sleep in the buff and once you get a full look"

I cut him off midsmarm. "You are *not* sleeping naked when we're in the same room."

He shrugs. "That's how I sleep."

"Not when we're in the same room. I have no desire to meet Dane Junior. That crosses a professional line and you know it."

"Fine, I'll keep my boxers on. Or do you want me to wear long-sleeve button-down jammies like a grandpa?"

I sort through my bag, looking for my toiletries and pajamas, which do happen to include pants and a long-sleeved shirt.

"No, I don't expect you to suddenly understand modesty," I answer lightly. "But make sure the boxers stay on at all times."

"Fine. While we're discussing ground rules, don't eat while I'm trying to sleep; it drives me nuts. And on game days, I take a nap in the afternoon, so don't wake me up or come in and out of the room then."

I toss my toiletry bag onto the bed and look over

at him. He's flossing his teeth, looking at his reflection in the mirrored closet doors.

"I'm a quiet roommate," I say. "I'll be asleep within ten minutes, and you should know that if I wake up at any point tonight and you aren't here, I'll call Tim. I'm not chasing you down in the middle of the night."

"I'm not going anywhere." He glares at me, aggravated. "Now, can I go take a shower, or do you want to follow me in there and tell me how to wash my balls?"

I'm so done with his quips. It's been a long day and I need some sleep.

"I need to get in the bathroom first; it'll take less than five minutes." I grab my toiletry bag and walk past him. "Then you can wash your balls however you want."

"Alone," he snaps. "I guess showering and sitting on the can are the only times I get to be alone anymore."

"You made your bed," I call out from the bathroom. "And now you want to bitch about having to lie in it."

He's silent, which is unlike him.

"You're flipping me off, aren't you?" I ask, the bathroom door still open.

"With both hands."

I close the bathroom door, quickly washing up and brushing my teeth. Then I crawl into bed without saying another word to Dane. Tomorrow is my first full day on the road with him, and something tells me I need to rest up for it.

seven

JOSIE

Jane: How are things going with the hockey player?

I stare at the phone screen for a second, considering telling the truth. But complaining never got anyone promoted. And since Dane is busy with his game day routine, today has been relatively peaceful for me.

Me: It's going well. He's getting ready for his game tonight.

Jane: Keep me apprised.

Classic Jane. She doesn't give compliments. *Keep me apprised* means I'm off the hook for now, but she could become displeased at any moment. I shove my phone back in my bag, glad I'm no longer under her watchful eye every day.

"Is this groin massage gonna have a happy ending?" a player named Tate McGovern asks as he gets on the athletic trainer's table.

"Probably," Gina, the trainer, answers with a shrug. "Seeing as I'm the only woman who ever touches you. Just keep quiet while you jizz in your pants, for fuck's sake."

Some of the players include Gina in their locker room banter; others don't. She doesn't take any shit from them. She said I could hang out with her in the training room, and in the hour I've been in here, I've learned a lot.

Apparently one of the Tampa players is going to get chirped at a lot tonight. They call him Smitty, and since he slept with a teammate's girlfriend, he's on his teammates' and his opponents' shit lists.

Chirping is trash-talking opponents on the ice. And from what the guys are saying about Smitty, he'll be hearing a lot of chirps about his small dick and his back acne tonight.

"Relax," Gina tells Tate as she puts on rubber gloves.

"How's Dane treating you, Josie?" Tate asks me.

Everyone calls him Tater. He's one of the friendliest members of the team, almost always smiling, unlike Dane, who's usually scowling.

"Fantastic," I deadpan.

"It's not your fault, you know. He's been a salty bastard since his divorce."

Record scratch. His divorce? Dane used to be *married?*

"When was that?" I ask.

"Uh, I think like four years ago?" He groans as Gina massages. "Damn, I feel like I should have taken you out for dinner before this."

She scoffs. "What, to White Castle?"

"That was one time," Tate says defensively. "It was after midnight and nothing else was open. It happened like two years ago, and my girlfriend at the time loved White Castle."

"I'd rather eat a stale bag of gas station peanuts than go to White Castle," Gina says, cringing. "Am I right, Josie?"

"I'd eat the plastic bag the peanuts came in before I ate White Castle."

Gina snort-laughs. "I think we're gonna be good friends."

"What should we call her?" Tate gives me a puzzled look. "Jo? JoJo?"

"Call her Josie," Gina says. "Save the nicknames for the boys."

"You're still not over me calling you Gina, are you?"

He pronounces it like *vagina*, and Gina shrugs. "I don't care, Tater. I know you're intellectually still in puberty, so I can see why it amuses you."

Dane walks into the room, announcing, "My back hurts."

"Can you be more specific?" Gina asks.

Dane furrows his brow in a textbook brood. "When I started stretching, I felt a twinge and it still hurts."

"How do you hurt yourself stretching?" Tate asks.

"Take a twenty-minute ice bath," Gina says. "Then I'll look at it."

Dane walks over to a big tub, which training assistants filled with ice earlier. He strips off his shirt and reaches for the waistband of his shorts.

"I'm out," I say, grabbing my bag.

"You don't want to see his bratwurst?" Tate asks, grinning.

"No."

"Aw, is our little Josie shy? Or have you never seen a pork sword before?"

I glare at him. "I've seen plenty, and if you refer to yours as a pork sword with women you're trying to get in bed, I get why Gina's the only woman who touches you."

"Tater's is more like a pork pocket knife," Dane says from the tub.

The sound of his deep voice makes me break out in goose bumps. There's something about knowing he's naked on the other side of the room I'm standing in right now that's unnerving.

"You get used to it after a while," Gina says. "They all look the same."

I shake my head, keeping my gaze on the door to the training room. She's still focused on the conversation, but the way my heart is racing, I'm focused on getting out of here.

I wasn't being completely honest with Tater when I said I've seen "plenty" of men naked.

Two. I've seen two. Sex with both of them was underwhelming, and neither of them ever made me break out in goose bumps the way Dane just did with his voice.

It's because I haven't even been kissed in more than a year. And because I'm in unfamiliar territory here. A pro sports locker room. It's not because I'm attracted to Dane.

He's attractive; that's more fact than opinion. But he ruins his good looks with his personality. I'm attracted to nice guys, not arrogant playboys.

Still, by the time I'm in the hallway outside the locker room, I feel like I'm the one who should be taking an ice bath.

"THAT'S HOW YOU DO IT, BABY!" JENN ROGERS jumps up from her seat and blows her husband a dozen flying kisses, alternating hands.

Aiden Rogers just scored a goal, and his teammates huddle around him in a circle to celebrate.

Aiden's name is announced and Dane is credited with an assist. Jenn lowers her brows and looks at me.

"Is Dane okay? He seems stiff."

"That's what she said," Elena says dismissively, her fingers flying over her phone, typing out a text.

"His back is sore," I say.

Elena sets down the phone and turns her attention back to me and Jenn. "Aaron says hotel beds are hard on his back sometimes. I find it so funny that he blames mattress firmness when he's sore after being boarded over and over in a game."

"Couldn't be the boarding," Jenn jokes. "He's too manly for that to hurt."

I'm sitting in a private box with around a dozen family members of players who made the trip to Tampa for the game.

"I heard you were sick on the plane," Elena says. "I get really bad motion sickness, too."

"Is there anything that helps it?"

"I know it sounds weird, but it helps me to eat something small before I fly. I take CBD oil, too. But if there's bad turbulence, I get sick anyway."

"Yeah, that flight felt like it took about twelve hours," I say. "I'm hoping to sleep on tonight's flight."

"Hope you can. I'm staying an extra couple of days at my hotel with my sister, my daughter and my two nephews. My sister's back at the hotel with the kids tonight."

"You have a daughter?"

She smiles brightly. "Amara. Now that you've indicated a slight interest, I have to break out my photo slideshow."

Elena's husband, Aaron, is tall and blond. Their daughter is a beautiful mix of the two of them with caramel curls and big dark-brown eyes. I ooh and aah at Elena's photos, trying not to let on how distracted I am by the conversation going on next to us.

"Of course Dane is tamable," a woman with flawless makeup and bright red nails says. "You just have to let him have his fun and always be there when he's done."

"I don't expect to be the only woman," another woman says. "I just want to be the only *legit* one, you know? The one in pictures with him."

"Exactly. I'm going to introduce you when the time is right. Just trust me."

I look over at Jenn and Elena to see if they heard the conversation. Jenn's completely focused on the game. Elena leans over and softly says, "We'll talk later."

I take Elena's advice and eat a soft pretzel. I'm nervous about flying again tonight, but it's inevitable. And this time, I'll be smarter and not sit next to Dane.

The Mammoths win the game 2–1. Dane has to do interviews afterward and then shower. I've been sitting on the floor in the hallway outside the locker room reading a book for more than an hour when he finally walks out of the locker room.

His hair is damp from the shower and he's dressed in a dark suit with a white dress shirt and a light-blue tie, his dress shoes shining. I feel frumpy next to him in my jeans, Vans and Mammoths T-shirt.

"Hey, Nosy," he says in greeting.

"Hi."

"Take this."

He holds out his hand and I put my outstretched palm under it. He drops a little white pill into my hand.

"Dramamine. Take it now."

"Oh." I look up at him, surprised. "Thanks."

"I just don't want to get puked on."

"Of course," I say wryly. "I didn't mean to insinuate you're considerate or anything."

He glares at me. "You're a pain in my ass, you know that?"

"Likewise, Foster."

His snoring woke me up last night and I couldn't get back to sleep for two hours. Then I woke up this morning to a bathroom that smelled like a long-neglected public sewer.

Hopefully Dane will be more bearable in Boston than he was in Tampa. Somehow, though, I doubt it.

eight

JOSIE

"She said to tell you she's sorry she had to work so much and that she loves you more than anything."

I sit up in bed with a gasp, my alarm waking me from a dream. After pushing a button on the screen to stop the alarm, I heave out a sigh, wishing I could fast-forward to bedtime.

It's March 11. Three years ago, on this day, my mom was killed by a drunk driver. I didn't make it to the hospital in time, so her final words to me were relayed by a nurse. Those words have haunted and comforted me since.

If only I could have told her not to feel guilty

over working two jobs from the time I was in fourth grade until I finished high school. My dad took off and left her as a single mom, and she did whatever it took to care for me, even though it left her very little time for herself.

I didn't get it as a child. Why she couldn't be at my dance recitals. Why we never took vacations. I get it now, and I admire my mom's resilience.

Dane walks out of the bathroom in a cloud of steam, a white towel wrapped around his waist. I force myself not to look because I don't want to get busted again.

"You need the bathroom?" he asks.

"Yes."

I gather my toiletries and clean clothes, trying to erase the mental image of the last time I saw my mom. The nurse told me seeing her body would give me closure, but it also gave me nightmares.

"I'm going down for breakfast," Dane says. "Are you coming to the morning skate?"

"Might as well."

"Bus leaves in thirty minutes."

I walk past him and into the bathroom, closing the door behind me. I press my back to the door and close my eyes, tears sliding down my cheeks.

The flight to Boston was a little better than the

Tampa flight, but I still threw up once and felt sick for most of it. We got to our hotel around four a.m., making the seven a.m. wake-up time feel downright offensive.

And now we get to do it all over again. After tonight's game, we'll fly to Seattle. I have to perk up because it's going to be a long day. Hopefully coffee and concealer will get me through.

I take a quick shower, dry my hair, put on light makeup and dress in black leggings, a maroon cami, a gray cardigan sweater and black flats.

I'm taking part in a Zoom meeting with everyone at my office later this morning, and this is as professional as I can look while living out of a backpack.

After packing my things, I walk down to the hotel dining room, where most of the team and staff are eating breakfast.

Dane is sitting at a table with two other players and I take the remaining seat. He's signing something for a little boy who's smiling at him like he's the greatest thing ever.

"Marco," the boy says.

"Marco, what position do you play?" Dane asks as he writes on a piece of paper.

"Defense and sometimes goalie," Marco says.

"Awesome. Keep your grades up, okay? And listen to your parents; they know what they're talking about."

Marco nods and a man waiting nearby asks if he can take a photo. Dane stands up and stands next to Marco, smiling for several photos.

"I guess we look like his assistants," Aiden mutters when Dane sits back down.

Dane grins. "Hey, if you want kids to ask for your autograph, try to suck less."

Aiden scoffs and glances at me. "Feeling any better, Josie?"

"Better than last night," I say. "Thanks."

I look at Dane, who has half a plate of scrambled eggs in front of him, the other half of the plate loaded with bacon, sausage and fruit. "Did you ask the housekeeper how Mr. Darcy's doing?"

Dane shrugs. "He's alive."

I glare at him across the table. "Is he eating? Does he seem anxious?"

"How's my housekeeper supposed to know if your cat is anxious?" He scoops a forkful of eggs into his mouth, sounding completely uninterested.

"I told you what to ask her, and instead, you asked if he's alive." I shake my head.

Aiden gestures toward the breakfast buffet. "You better eat. We're out of here in five minutes."

I grab a muffin and some yogurt from the buffet and head for the bus, not in the mood to watch Dane feed his face.

The bus takes us to a small arena where the team does a pregame skate and then to the downtown Boston arena where the team is playing tonight. Dalton and Dane are both stopped by reporters shortly after stepping off the bus, and I linger nearby so I can hear Dane's interview.

"Dane, Boston has a four-game winning streak going. How will you approach playing them tonight?"

Dane grins at the beautiful female reporter. "We beat 'em last time we were here. If we stay focused, I think we'll walk away with another win."

"Have you heard about Abigail Matthews, the fan who's trending on social media with the hashtag *datemedane*?"

"No clue about that."

"She's a law student at the University of Chicago who wants you to take her out on a date."

He smiles. "I'm flattered, but right now, I have to focus on tonight's game and the ones we have coming up. We've got a tough stretch ahead and we need to keep our eye on the ball."

"Thanks, Dane. Good luck tonight." She flashes him her million-dollar smile and he nods.

If anyone's ego *wasn't* in need of a boost, it's Dane. But of course, as I trail behind him entering the arena, I'm searching the hashtag the reporter mentioned.

FFS. Abigail Matthews is a stunning redhead. She's pictured in one of the posts at a Mammoths game, looking radiant in a jersey with Dane's number on it.

Dane stops walking and turns around, waiting for me to catch up.

"Hey, could you drop off some dry cleaning at a one-hour place for me today?" he asks.

"I don't know...could you pick up some tampons and lube for me?"

"Fuck no," he says, wrinkling his nose.

"I'm not your assistant."

He rolls his eyes. "I know. I just thought since you'll be here for the next ten hours or so, you could do an errand for me."

"You thought wrong."

He scowls. "You come off all cute and helpful, but you're kind of a viper, Nosy."

Better a viper than a doormat. But more importantly...he thinks I'm cute?

"I'm here to do the job I was assigned."

He arches a brow. "Do you really need lube? Do you have an issue with dryness down there?"

My face burns with embarrassment. "No. I don't need tampons, either. It was just an example."

"Sure it was." He winks at me. "Don't worry, I won't tell."

I want to shove him aside like the annoyance he is, but if I tried, it would be like trying to push over a brick wall. He walks into the locker room and I follow.

Gina said she'd help me find a room for my Zoom meeting, so I find her and put Dane out of my mind. I'm looking forward to my meeting, where I can be reminded I have job skills other than shadowing an obnoxious hockey player.

THE MAMMOTHS LOST TO BOSTON, 3–2. THE mood on the bus to the airport is gloomy. Most of the guys have headphones on.

This bus is small, and nearly every seat is filled. I have to sit next to Dane instead of sitting alone, and he's spent the entire ride so far texting. His jaw is set and his expression is pissed off as his fingers fly over the phone screen.

Who is he texting? I'm dying to know, but I can't get even a peek at his screen.

He passed me a Dramamine when he walked out of the locker room, not saying a word. I'm assuming he's angry about losing the game like the rest of the team seems to be.

It's like a completely different group than last night. No one is talking or laughing.

I thought I'd be exhausted after getting so little sleep last night, but I was busy all day at the arena and I'm still running on adrenaline. I had my Zoom meeting, caught up on work emails and helped a Mammoths PR person who needed me to coordinate some things with the Boston PR people.

Keeping busy was a blessing because I didn't have time to think about my mom. Even after three years, it still hurts. I hope the day comes when I can remember the good times and smile when I think about her.

Dane turns the power off on his phone, sighing heavily.

"Everything okay?" I ask.

"Fucking awesome," he says angrily.

"Great."

He glares at me. "The reason I needed my dry cleaning taken in is because you puked on my shirt the other night."

"Oh yeah? Is that why you're so pissed off right now?"

It takes him a couple of seconds to respond. "Might be."

"So if I take your dry cleaning in tomorrow, will you stop being such a dick?"

"Maybe."

"You're projecting. You're mad at someone else and you're trying to make me think it's about your shirt."

"Thanks, Dr. Phil."

My stomach turns as I think about getting on an airplane yet again. I don't have much fight in me right now.

"I'll take your dry cleaning in tomorrow. Only because I don't have a busy day and because I'm a nice person. It doesn't mean I'm your errand girl."

"Thanks."

I glance at him. "So I looked into that hashtag thing the reporter mentioned, and as your PR representative, I feel like I should tell you it's trending majorly. And since I'm here to help rebuild your image, I think you should consider taking that woman on a date."

He groans. "No. I don't have time, and I don't like clingy women."

"Just one date. One dinner. You show up in a suit with flowers and take her out to dinner and that's it. The internet would love it."

"I'll think about it," he says, his tone indicating that he won't.

The bus stops at the airport and everyone starts gathering up headphones and bottled drinks.

Whether or not my stomach is ready, we're heading to Seattle.

nine

JOSIE

"One java chip frap."

I pass Gina the drink I got her on my Starbucks run and she gives me a grateful look.

"I'm naming my firstborn after you. I couldn't sleep on the plane because of Parker's snoring."

We're in the training room at the Seattle arena; puck drop still a few hours away. I got lucky last night—I was so tired I fell asleep against the plane window shortly after sitting down and didn't wake up until the plane was descending. Of course, I threw up immediately, but it was only twenty minutes of misery, which is progress.

Dalton walks into the training room and gives Gina an expectant look.

"Are you gonna wrap my ankle?"

"Yeah, get on the table."

Dalton nods at me in greeting. "Thanks for asking if I wanted Starbucks, Josie."

Gina rolls her eyes. "Leave her alone. Coffee gives you the shits, D. Remember that time you didn't make it to the bathroom in time in Dallas?"

"One doesn't forget shitting one's self."

I take out my laptop to check my email and fall down a rabbit hole, helping a colleague write a proposal for a potential new client. While Gina wraps, massages and ices players, I spend nearly three hours typing on my computer while sitting in a folding chair.

My back protests when I finally stand up and stretch.

"I'm going to the bathroom. Do you need anything?" I ask Gina.

"No, thanks."

The Mammoths goalie, Lucas Robinson, comes into the training room wearing his bulky gear.

"Hey, Josie," he says.

"Hey."

"What's up with you?" Gina asks him as I leave the room.

I have to walk through the locker room to get to the bathroom, and when I glance over at Dane, he's engaged in a heated conversation with Tim, his coach.

"Prove yourself with your play," Tim says earnestly. "Let go of the past."

Dane shakes his head, his brow lined with aggravation. "I won't start shit with him, but if he starts it, I'll damn well finish it."

Tim rubs his forehead. "That approach lands you in the box every time. I know there's bad blood between the two of you, but"

"You don't know," Dane says angrily. "Until it happens to you, you have no idea."

I walk into the bathroom, wondering what they're talking about. By the time I walk back out, Dane is sitting with his back against the wall, wearing headphones. His eyes are closed and it's clear he doesn't want to be disturbed.

Back in the training room, Gina is looking through the bag of supplies she takes to the bench for games, and Lucas is sitting in the folding chair I was in before.

"Hey, Josie," he says, standing.

He's never spoken to me until today, but from everything I've heard, he's a nice guy. He has longish blond hair with loose curls and warm brown eyes.

"Hi, Lucas, how's it going?"

"It's good. Always gotta be on our toes in Seattle."

I approach to pack my laptop and cord into my bag. "They have a really nice arena here."

"Yeah, it's one of the best." He clears his throat. "So I heard you get sick on the plane. Are you feeling okay?"

"I'm good. I actually slept for most of the flight last night."

He clears his throat again. "That's good. You look, you know, well rested."

"Lucas fucking Robinson!" someone yells from the locker room.

He glances in that direction and gives me a sheepish grin. "Duty calls. I'll catch you later."

"Yeah, have a good game."

"Thanks."

He leaves the room and I finish packing my things. Gina gives me a knowing smile.

"What?" I ask.

"He's really shy. So sweet, though. He likes you."

"What? No."

She laughs. "You're blind if you didn't notice. He didn't need anything from me. He only came in here to see you."

I'm pretty sure Lucas was just being nice. Trying to make me feel welcome. Which is nice, but doesn't mean he's interested in me.

"I'm going to find my seat," I say.

Gina sighs dramatically. "Enjoy the buffet up there. Eat some crab legs for me. I'll be having a soggy sub sandwich."

Tonight, I'm sitting with the team owner, Arnold. Before every game, someone from the Mammoths' PR department texts me to tell me where I'll be sitting. I haven't eaten since I wolfed down a little food before catching the bus this morning, so a buffet sounds great.

"You get a better view of the game, though," I say.

"True. I have to smell the stank hockey gear, though."

I want to ask her if she knows what Tim and Dane were talking about earlier. If Dane has a beef with someone from the Seattle team, I need to know about it. It could lead to negative headlines.

It's too late, though. Interns and equipment people are coming in and out of the room. I'll have to ask her another time.

"See you later," I tell Gina.

"Later, Josie."

ARNOLD WALKS INTO THE VIP BOX JUST BEFORE puck drop, shaking hands and chatting with his invited guests. I'm glad to be sitting alone in the corner of the box, because it allows me to focus on the game.

I had no idea how exciting hockey was until I started this assignment. It's fast paced, the energy of it unlike any sport I've ever watched.

From my seat, I can see all the action. Dane came out charging tonight, playing more aggressively than anyone else on the ice. It pays off when he slides a puck into the net, colliding with another player while scoring a goal.

The celebration in the box is low key, most people immediately going back to their conversations. I return my attention to the game, following the players and the puck up and down the ice over and over. There are a few close shots, but no other goals are scored before the end of the first period.

Arnold approaches me during the break, extending his hand for me to shake.

"How are you, Josie?"

"Hi, Arnold, I'm great," I say, shaking his hand.

"Is Dane treating you okay?"

I smile. "I can handle myself when he's temperamental."

He grins. "Jane said you've got the backbone to handle him. I've learned over the years to trust her judgment."

My aunt said that about me? I'm flattered but also stunned. All my performance reviews focus on what I need to improve on. There are never compliments.

"I hear Dane is trending on social media for something other than bad behavior," Arnold says. "So you're doing a great job."

I'm not doing much, but I don't argue with Arnold. I've endured too much air sickness and lack of sleep to tell him it was nothing.

"Oh, the law student who wants a date with him?" I ask.

"Yes."

"I think he should do it."

"Sure, our PR people could even set everything up," he says.

The players return to the ice, the crowd roaring as music booms.

"We need this win," Arnold says. "It's crunch time."

I squint at one of the screens in the arena, making out the words on the cardboard sign a fan is holding up.

It says *Marry Me Lucas.* Sweet. I read another one.

Shaw doesn't need a penalty to get in my box.

WTF? The camera quickly pans to another set of fans. Shaw must be a Seattle player. Looks like Dane isn't the only one with thirsty female fans.

The game resumes and Arnold sits down in the open seat next to me. We watch the game in silence for a couple of minutes, but when Dane gets shoved by a Seattle player between plays, Arnold groans.

Dane immediately throws his gloves off. My heart pounds hard as he throws a punch at another player. Fans jump to their feet, yelling as the two men fight.

I look at Arnold, wondering why this is being

allowed. Aren't the referees supposed to stop it? Dane's getting the better end of the fight, but he's taken several blows to the head.

The Seattle player says something that causes Dane to shove him to the ice and climb on top of him, punching him repeatedly. Players from both teams jump into the fight, the referees trying to break it up with no luck.

"Dammit," Arnold mutters, burying his face in his hands.

Finally, the refs break the fight up, fans screaming as a ref points at Dane and he skates away.

"What happened?" I ask.

"He was ejected."

Dane is almost off the ice when he says something to a fan who's yelling at him from the stands. The fan flips him the double bird and Dane opens his arms and says, "Come on! Let's go!"

"Dane, stop," I say softly.

"Nothing gets him going like Sam Styles," Arnold says, typing out a text on his phone.

"Is that the Seattle player who started the fight?"

He nods. "I don't know who started it, but Dane

can't play this team without a major altercation with Styles."

"Why?"

He looks over his shoulder to make sure no one is in earshot, then speaks in a low tone. "His wife left him for Sam. It's been years, but..." He shrugs. "I don't think a man ever forgives that. They were teammates when it happened."

"Oh my God."

I sit back in my seat, stunned. The conversation between Dane and Tim makes sense now.

"Don't even try to talk to him," Arnold cautions. "I hear he's impossible to be around after one of these fights."

I sigh heavily. "I wish I'd known about this."

He gives me a small smile. "You couldn't have done anything about it, Josie. It's going to be like this until one of them retires."

"What does this mean? He got ejected from the game, is that it?"

"We'll know more soon."

I gather up my things. "I'm going to talk to him."

Without waiting for Arnold to tell me not to, I leave the VIP box, my heart still racing. I have to flash my all-access badge at least a dozen times before I get into the locker room, and when I do, I inhale sharply as I lay eyes on Dane.

The team doctor is examining him in the training room. Both of his eyes are swollen, one nearly closed, and he has a fat lip. There's a distant look in his eyes.

"I need to sew up the eyebrow," the doctor says.

I let the doctor work, a training assistant passing him things as he needs them. When he takes a break to wash the blood from his hands, I approach Dane.

"Not now," he says, not even looking at me.

I nod, unable to feel angry at him. His wife cheated on him with a teammate. It explains so much.

It also leaves me with a thousand questions. None of which will be answered anytime soon.

ten

DANE

"You're suspended for two games," Tim says from the other side of the conference table. "I called in a lot of favors to keep it from being three."

"Thanks, Coach."

I can't make myself look remorseful because I'm not. If I had to do it over again, I'd stop my fist from connecting with a ref's shoulder, but I wouldn't change anything else. The ref shouldn't have inserted himself between me and Styles when I was midpunch.

"This isn't a great look, but it's a step up from

the park bench incident," says Tamara Curtis, the head of the Mammoths PR department.

Her tone has its usual edge. Only the guys who spend their off days inoculating orphans and rescuing cats from trees get her friendly voice. I'll consider myself a failure at life if Tamara ever likes me.

"Josie, maybe you need to be out on the ice with him from now on," Tamara says, sighing.

Tamara was the one who called this meeting, and so far, the only agenda item is berating me. My fucking head hurts and I slept like shit on the flight home. So I'm extra not in the mood to be sitting in this conference room with my coach, Josie and Tamara. It's Tamara's job to recommend how I spend my time while suspended. And if she thinks I'm volunteering at a food pantry on no sleep with this raging headache, she's dead wrong.

"I don't think it's that big of a deal," Josie says. "I've been keeping up with hockey headlines and everyone seems to understand that Dane wasn't aiming for the ref. The ref just got in the way, but the rules are the rules and he had to be suspended. Fans love that Dane is a fighter. It's part of the game and he doesn't back down."

I look at her, momentarily stunned. She just stood up for me, even though I was a complete dick to her on the flight home. I bitched about her cat, her taste in music and the light from her phone, but none of it was really about her. She knew that because she took it all in stride instead of fighting back like usual.

Tamara turns her sharp gaze on Josie.

"We don't glamorize fighting and suspensions. Have you seen the pictures of Sam Styles's face?"

Josie shrugs. "It's hockey, not badminton."

I sneak a glance at Tim. My coach's lips are quirking with a smile. Josie is a quick study. She didn't just show up and follow me around; she immersed herself in listening and learning about the game, the players and the fans. She gets it in a way Tamara never will, and Tamara has worked for the Mammoths for years.

"Listen, Tamara," Tim says. "We just got in from a long night of travel. I'd like to wrap this up as quickly as possible."

Tamara nods and looks down at her notepad. "Will you consider an apology?"

I scoff. "Absolutely not."

Josie speaks up. "I think Dane should attend the

games he's suspended from to support his team. He can stop by the VIP boxes to meet fans. I also want to get him to the children's hospital to meet the boy with cancer who started a Twitter campaign wanting to meet him."

I don't pay attention to social media, and I immediately feel guilty that a kid with cancer has been trying to meet me and I had no idea.

"Done," I say. "But what if Josie wasn't here? Isn't it the team PR office's job to know about that stuff? I don't want people to think I blow off kids with cancer."

Tamara's eyes bulge. "Since when have you cared about your image?"

I look at Tim. "Isn't it literally her job to be on top of things like that?"

Tim's expression tells me he wants me to stop aggravating her so we can all get the hell out of here. Tamara's like a wind-up toy fully wound now.

"We're short-staffed and it's all we can do to keep up with our regular work. If you want to know what's happening with your social media, I suggest you look at it."

Josie puts up a hand. "I'm here to look at it, and I am. Let's stay focused."

Tamara huffs out a sigh. "I need to clarify some

things with Arnold. Now that Dane has a personal publicist, maybe the PR department needs to step away from things involving him."

She might as well hiss and break out her claws. Josie cocks her head and meets my gaze for a brief second and I instinctively wink at her, silently telling her I get it.

"I don't want you to step away," Josie says. "I'd like us to work together."

"I heard you think Dane should go on a date with a college student," Tamara says. "Don't you think college girls are too young for him?"

"She's actually a law student. She's twenty-four and he's twenty-eight. I think it's fine."

Tamara sniffs. "Well, prepare for an onslaught of bad press when he dumps her and she's on TikTok crying her eyes out."

"Just one date," Josie says. "He'll be friendly." She shoots me a look. "With some coaching beforehand, I mean. There would be photos of the two of them smiling and having dinner. She's not expecting a marriage proposal. She just wants to meet him."

Josie stood up for me when I didn't deserve it, and I want to return the favor.

"I'll do it," I say.

"Heaven help us," Tamara mutters. "Don't get yourself handcuffed to another park bench."

Tim stands up. "I think we're done here."

Tamara stands too, not even looking at me or Josie as she says, "Thank you for your time, Coach."

One of the equipment people loads our bags into my car, leaving my keys on the car seat, so Josie and I start our walk to the players' parking garage. Tim waves at us and heads toward the front office.

Josie looks over at me and smiles. "I think she likes me."

"Not as much as she likes me," I quip.

I WAKE UP AND REACH FOR MY PHONE ON THE nightstand, my eyelids heavy.

It's 5:42. A.m. or pm., I have no idea. I don't even know for sure what day it is, but thanks to my suspension, it's no big deal either way.

I get up and use the bathroom, then head for the kitchen. A savory garlic smell makes my stomach rumble. I'm thirsty as hell and hungry, too.

When I make it to the kitchen, I see Josie

standing in front of the stove, her hair up in a big bun on top of her head. She's wearing a gray tank top and black leggings, and my gaze wanders up and down her back, admiring the view.

Josie is pretty. I knew that the first time I saw her. But it's not her looks making me feel drawn to her right now. Well...it's not *just* her looks. I'm not blind.

I like that she doesn't take an ounce of shit from me in private, but she publicly stands up for me. Who knows if she'd treat me that way if she wasn't being paid to be here, but it feels good.

"Hey, sorry I woke you up," she says, turning around to face me. "I dropped a pan."

"It's okay. Is it evening or morning?"

She smiles. "It's evening. We got back here at eight thirty this morning. I slept until three thirty and I was starving for real food when I woke up, so I checked the fridge. It's full of fresh vegetables and other stuff that wasn't there when we left. What is this sorcery?"

"My housekeeper." I walk over to a cabinet to get a glass.

"Nice. Well, I'm making a huge veggie stir-fry if you're hungry."

"I am. Thanks."

I go over to the fridge and fill my glass from the water dispenser, drinking two full glasses before I sit down at the island.

"Am I supposed to offer to help?"

With a single note of laughter, she says, "Spoken like someone who definitely does not want to help."

"I'm no good in the kitchen."

She pops a broccoli floret into her mouth and stirs the food. "Okay, I have a noncooking job for you."

"What is it?"

"Change Mr. Darcy's litter."

I scoff. "Not a chance in hell, Nosy."

"I was joking. I want you to send a message to Abigail Matthews."

"Who?"

"The law student who wants to go out with you."

I groan, not in the mood to be fake friendly until I've at least eaten. A shot of whiskey would help, too.

"I'll tell you what to write," she says. "Find her on TikTok."

I open the app. "Abigail Matthews?"

"Yep."

"This is gonna be a pain in my ass."

Josie sets a steaming plate of stir fry in front of me. "Why?"

"Because she goes by Abigail. Why not Abby? Same with Tamara. Just go by Tammy like a normal fucking person."

Josie smiles wryly and makes a plate for herself, standing on the other side of the island to eat.

"Alright, I found her," I say.

"Write this: Hey Abigail, it's Dane."

I look up at her, furrowing my brow. "It's my account, of course it's me."

"So she knows it's not from one of your people. Just write it like I'm telling you, okay?"

"Fine," I grumble, typing out the message.

"I'll be in Chicago in a couple of weeks for a game, want to grab some dinner?" she continues.

"Don't ask me to use the word 'cheers' at the end. I'm not doing it."

She rolls her eyes. "You're such a man-child. Just leave it like it is and send it."

I finish the message and set my phone aside, digging into my food.

"This is actually really good," I say.

"Of course it is. I'm a woman of many talents."

Her confidence is hot. I try to figure out if she's wearing a bra. No visible nip, so probably.

Damn. If she weren't wearing a bra, that would mean she was trying to get me to look. Even though we don't get along, today feels like a truce of sorts.

Who knows what tomorrow will bring, though?

eleven

JOSIE

IF I DIDN'T KNOW HOW MOODY AND ARROGANT HE could be, I'd think Dane Foster was an absolute saint. A stand-up guy. A gentleman, even.

Archie Bright, the nine-year-old cancer patient who just met Dane for the first time, is looking at him with such reverence that it takes my breath away. When we arrived, he cried and hugged Dane for a solid five minutes and he's just now managed to let go of him so they can have a conversation, both of them wearing masks.

This morning, Dane called my cat "a furry menace" and griped at me for not emptying the lint trap in his dryer. Then he made me a delicious cheese omelet. I still haven't figured out if he's mercurial or just constantly trying to balance out his grouchiness with good deeds.

Right now, though, I'm in awe of him. Archie is bald and thin, and he was staring listlessly at nothing in his hospital bed when we walked into the room. Now his eyes are shining happily and he's holding Dane's hand. Dane is smiling warmly at the little boy, listening to him talk about watching hockey games on TV.

"They don't have most of the Mammoths' games on TV here," he says glumly. "Sometimes they do, though."

"How would you feel about watching tomorrow night's game against Chicago?" Dane asks.

Archie lights up. "Oh yeah! I'm watching that one. Regina said I can stay up late and watch it on the big TV in the lounge. She's one of my nurses."

Dane shakes his head and makes a face, looking at Archie's mom, Taylor.

"I don't think you guys should let him stay up late and watch it in the lounge," he says.

"What?" Archie cries.

Dane waves a hand dismissively. "If you've seen one hockey game, you've seen 'em all, man."

"No!" Archie's expression is devastated. "I want to watch the game! Regina said I can!"

"How about this?" Dane says. "You can still watch the game, but instead of watching it from the lounge here, you come to the arena and watch it with me in person."

The little boy's eyes fill with happy tears and he looks at his mom. "Can I?"

His mom is smiling through tears as she says, "Of course, baby."

It's a good thing the Mammoths' PR office sent two of their photographers with us to capture this meeting on video and in photos because I can't keep it together anymore. I have to step out of the room to go clean my tear-streaked face off in the bathroom.

Archie and his family deserve all the joy in the world. All I asked Dane to do was come here and meet Archie, but he asked Arnold for a private area where he, Archie and his family could watch a game. He'd read through posts Archie's mom had put on social media and knew steering clear of germs was important for him. That's why Arnold is giving up his own private box for tomorrow night's game and having it disinfected from top to bottom so Archie and his family will have a safe place to watch.

I take a short walk, get a Diet Coke from a vending machine and put my mask back on before returning to Archie's room, where Dane is crouched down next to his bed.

"Does it hurt when you get hit by a puck?" Archie asks him.

"Not too bad. Unless you catch a puck to the old coin purse without pads on."

Archie laughs, his hand still holding firmly to Dane's.

"Who's your favorite player of all time?" Archie asks him.

"All time?" Dane considers.

"Mine is a tie between you and Gretzky."

Dane grins. "Wow. I don't compare to him, but I'm honored."

"Sometimes Regina lets me hit pucks down the hallway when everyone's asleep."

A young woman in scrubs on the other side of the room laughs. "Archie, that was supposed to be our secret."

The photographers take several photos of Dane and Archie and then more with Archie's parents and younger brother. Then Archie asks if he can show Dane the room where he watches the games, which turns into a tour of the whole floor and Dane meeting and taking photos with several other patients.

He's the best version of himself when interacting with the kids. Kind and funny. Most importantly, he listens to them. He never rushes them or acts disinterested in what they're saying. It's hard to believe this is the same guy Arnold referred to as "a PR nightmare" when he hired me.

"That was fun," Dane says to me when we're leaving the hospital after being there for nearly three hours, and I can tell he means it.

"You were great," I say.

"That's one thing I never mind doing." He glances away and then back at me. "My younger sister had cystic fibrosis."

I have to process that for a few seconds before I can respond. He said *had*. Past tense.

"I'm so sorry," I say.

He shrugs. "It's a brutal fucking disease. So is cancer. If I can do anything to brighten a kid's day when they're fighting a battle like that, it's a tiny thing. Nothing compared to what they go through."

I nod as an elevator takes us down to the hospital's main entrance, a lump in my throat. His suspension turned out to be a blessing in disguise. Dane's time with Archie today was more important than any hockey practice or game.

A FEW HOURS LATER, I'M TAKING MR. DARCY'S blanket out of the dryer when Dane calls out from the kitchen.

"I need to get out of the house. I'm bored as fuck."

So much for my evening plans of catching up on work, ordering pizza and reading.

"Okay, I just need to take a quick shower before we leave," I said. "But first, I have to empty the lint trap because that's critically important to me."

"It is important, Nosy!"

I roll my eyes as I take the tiny amount of lint and hair from the trap and carry it into the kitchen to throw away. Then I return Mr. Darcy's blanket to my bed and walk into the kitchen, where Dane's eating crackers.

"Where do you want to go?" I ask him.

He shrugs. "Someplace low key."

I walk over to the refrigerator to get my water

bottle, Dane making no effort to move out of the way as I brush past him. I'd be embarrassed for anyone to know how hard my heart pounds when we're so close I can feel the heat of his body. I'm here to do a job, but I'm still human, and it's been a long time since I was in close quarters with an attractive man.

"Anyone ever tell you you've got great legs?" he asks casually.

His compliment makes my mouth go dry. I'm wearing shorts and a T-shirt, my hair up in a ponytail. I love that he was looking at me, but it also makes me feel a little panicked.

"Um...I don't know," I say.

No. The answer is *no*. No one has ever told me that, but it's hard to be coherent right now.

We're standing just a couple of feet away from each other, both of us leaning against the kitchen island counter. He stopped eating, his gaze now fixed on...my lips? My eyes? I feel the heavy, pleasant weight of his attention all over.

"I can see why Lucas has the hots for you," he says.

"Who?"

The corners of his lips turn up in a smile. "Right answer. He's our goalie."

"Oh." I clear my throat, forcing my gaze away from his.

My eyes land on one of his hands. It's resting on the island and it's enormous. My mind wanders to what it would feel like to have that hand running up my thigh. His hands are so big that he could cup my entire ass in both of them.

"Go take your shower so we can go out," he says, winking.

"Okay."

Suddenly, going out doesn't sound so bad anymore. I turn on a playlist and shower with my favorite coconut shower gel, moving quickly. Afterward, I cover myself in lotion, telling myself it's just because I want to and not because I don't want dry skin if Dane happens to...encounter any of my skin later.

I can't let anything happen between us. It would undermine my professional relationship with him. I've seen colleagues lose credibility with clients over personal relationships. Jane even lost a big client once when her relationship with their company's CEO went bad.

A night out won't hurt anything, though. Maybe there'll be some flirting, but as long as we each go to our own beds after returning home, it's okay.

It's a good thing I spent some money on new clothes that arrived here while we were gone for our road trip. I wouldn't have wanted to pull something wrinkled out of my backpack for tonight.

After dressing in formfitting black pants, a silky dark-green cap-sleeved top and low, strappy black heels, I put on light makeup and walk back into the kitchen.

"Dane?" I call out.

When he doesn't respond, I check his bedroom and bathroom, which are both empty. I walk back out to the living room, wondering where the hell he went.

My heart skips a beat when I see a note taped to the back of the front door. My heels click against the wood floors as I walk over to read it.

I need a night out alone. Don't worry about me.
Dane

I read it three times, my heart sinking a little more each time. Tears of frustration fill my eyes.

He played me. He turned on the fake charm and pretended to like me, all so he could bolt as soon as I got in the shower. And I fell for it like a complete idiot.

I'm angry, but more than that, I'm humiliated.

What a fool I was, moisturizing myself for him while he was laughing and driving away.

I can't even go look for him because I have no idea where he went. Slipping out of my heels, I send texts to Jenn and Elena, telling them to let me know if they hear about Dane being out somewhere.

If he gets into trouble, we're both sunk. He's suspended, and it's especially important that he not be seen out partying right now.

Not that he cares. The one and only thing Dane Foster cares about is himself.

I won't forget that again.

twelve

DANE

"Another?" the bartender asks me, almost sounding impressed at this point.

I get it. I'm also surprised I'm still upright on the barstool. I've been here for hours, drowning every emotion in whiskey before it has a chance to surface.

Feelings bad. Whiskey good. That mantra has gotten me through the past four years, so why mess with it now?

"Did I mention she has great legs?"

Marti, the bartender, nods as she refills my shot glass. "A couple of times."

I've been talking to Marti since the bar cleared out around eleven p.m. She's a married mom of two adult kids, so I don't have to worry she'll think I'm trying to pick her up.

"Last one, Fred. And I'm not letting you walk out of here and get into a car, just so you know."

I give her a foolish grin, wondering what the hell I was so wound about when I got here. "My name's not really Fred. Shh."

"You don't say."

I tip back the shot glass and set it on the wood bar top. "You know your shit, Marti. Ain't nobody gettin' a lie by you, is they?"

"Not a chance." She uses a white towel to dry a tall glass. "So you like this woman, but you also don't like her, right?"

I cringe as I consider the question. "She drives me crazy like...eighty-seven point forty-two percent of the time. But the other fifty percent..." I put my hands out in front of me, trying to demonstrate...something. "I just want to push her onto the bed and...you know what I'm sayin'?"

"Yep."

She puts the glass back on a shelf and takes another one from the sink of soapy water.

"Is my ass still on the barstool?" I ask.

"For the moment."

Marti pours a glass of water from a pitcher and sets it in front of me. "Drink it, Fred."

I look at the glass. "I'm not ready."

"Not ready for what? That awful feeling when you *don't* pass out and hit your head on something?"

"She's gonna be so mad at me."

Marti laughs. "Who, Legs? Judging by the amount of whiskey you just put away, I'm guessing she already knows drinking is an issue for you."

Reluctantly, I pick up the glass and take a drink of the icy water.

I made Josie think we were going out together and then ditched her. She's going to be furious at me, and I understand why. She started to trust me and got burned.

"Tell me you didn't just break a sobriety streak," Marti says. "I would've tried to talk you out of that if I'd known."

I laugh and say, "No. I ditched Nosy."

"You ditched her? Why? It sounds like you really like her."

I drink more of the water, reality starting to seep back in.

"That's just it, Marti. It's *it*. I'm no good."

She puts another glass away. "Why do you think that?"

"Let's see..." I put a finger out. "One, I'm cold. And two...I'm an asshole." I look at my fingers, getting confused. Might as well just put all ten fingers up. "Too possessive. But that's number three, not two."

Marti nods. "So a past girlfriend told you these things and now you think you're no good."

"She was right, though." I rest my elbow on the bar, putting my forehead in my palm. "I get jealous. I even got jealous when I heard Lucas likes Nosy."

"And Nosy is Legs, right?"

"Yep."

"Here's my advice. Stop calling her Nosy, for Christ's sake. Man up and tell her how you feel."

Marti refills my water glass and I meet her gaze across the bar.

"You're a nice one, Marti."

She laughs. "I'm just blunt, Fred. And trust me, no one fucks up the way you feel about yourself like an ex. I have a horrible ex in my past. He made me question everything about myself. You seem like a good guy who's afraid to get hurt again. But no risk, no reward."

"Word. I think I better get to my bathroom."

"You feelin' the urge to purge?"

"Yeah, where's my bathroom?"

She comes around the bar and helps me off the barstool. "I'll show you where you're going. And the good news is, it probably smells like piss and vomit, so it'll make you puke real quick like. Makes me want to puke and I don't even drink."

"You're a riot," I say, trying not to lean on her because I'm huge and she's wiry. "We should hang out."

"I'm here from seven p.m. to two a.m. five nights a week."

Marti leaves me at the bathroom door and I go inside. She's right. The smell sends my stomach over the edge and I barely make it to the toilet to throw up.

Twenty minutes later, my stomach is empty and Marti is using my phone to call an Uber.

"You can have my car," I say. "It's really nice."

She chuckles. "If I took all the things customers offer me when they're drunk, I could retire."

When my ride arrives, she walks outside with me to make sure I get in. I turn to her and open my arms.

"I feel like we should hug. Some breakthroughs happened here tonight."

"Just get in the car, Fred. This will all be a blur tomorrow."

"I love you."

She laughs. "You made this night a lot more fun; I'll tell you that much."

I crawl into the back seat of the Uber and lie down.

"Don't puke in my car," the driver cautions from the front seat.

"I won't."

Judging by the swirling sensation in my stomach, I may be overpromising on that.

I SNEAK THROUGH MY FRONT DOOR, GENTLY closing it and tiptoeing across the darkened room.

"Where the hell have you been?"

A furious Josie jumps off the couch and I sigh heavily.

"You scared the shit out of me."

"Oh, did I? You can wait the rest of your life for me to apologize. I spent hours looking for you. Calling hospitals. Praying whatever mess you got into won't get out and cost both of us our jobs."

It sounds like she's speaking to me from the inside of my ear. I take a few steps away.

"Look, can we talk tomorrow?"

Even in the dark, I see her eyes flash with fury.

"You're drunk. Why am I even surprised? You smell like a distillery. Please tell me you didn't get naked in public tonight."

I take a few more steps toward my bedroom door. "I'll tell you tomorrow."

"You really disappointed me tonight, Dane."

The catch in her voice makes me stop walking and hang my head. I'd take her fury over this any day. I want to tell her it's not what she thinks, that I didn't do any of this to hurt her.

I can't, though.

"We'll talk about it tomorrow," I say, changing course to walk into the kitchen. "I just want to get some water and go to bed."

She follows me. "If anything happened tonight that could bite us in the ass tomorrow, I need to know about it now. Please."

"Nothing happened."

I down a glass of water from the fridge dispenser and fill it again.

"No fights? No sleeping with anyone's wife? No encounters with law enforcement?"

I glare at her. "I said no. I had a few drinks alone at a bar."

"You are so lucky I didn't call Tim," she says, her voice thick with emotion. "That's what I'm supposed to do. This is supposed to be your last chance."

Her silhouette is beautiful, her hair hanging loose and her hourglass shape outlined in the dim light. I can't break down and tell her the truth— that my attraction to her is why I had to get away for a few hours.

"Go to bed, Josie. I'll see you tomorrow."

"I hope you have nightmares about rats eating your ball sac," she says bitterly.

I'm close to laughing when a wave of nausea hits and I have to race to the bathroom. I can't puke in front of Josie. That would make a shitty situation even worse.

I can't get to my toilet, but I make it to my shower. Since no one but me and my housekeeper come in here, I can deal with the mess tomorrow morning.

For now, all I manage is to wipe off my face with a wet washcloth and fall face-first into bed.

thirteen

JOSIE

"Hey, man," Dane says to Archie, giving him a fist bump as he and his family arrive for the game.

Archie is beaming as he passes Dane a picture he drew of the two of them.

"You didn't tell me you were an artist," Dane says. "This is great."

He asks one of the PR people to get him a folder to keep his picture safe in, and I remind myself that I'm mad at him. It's hard to stay that way, though, as I watch Dane and Archie posing for photos, both of them in masks. Dane made sure there was an entire box of medical masks in the suite and had a sign put on the door saying no one could enter without one on.

I'm only speaking to him when I have to. I'd rather unleash my fury, but this is a working relationship and I need to keep it professional. The silent treatment seems to be driving him crazy, but he brought it on himself.

While everyone else watches the game, I'm in a corner of the suite on my laptop. My biggest client at work is a cable company called Brightside, and I didn't want to shift the account to another publicist during the Dane assignment and risk never getting it back. I'm working with Julie, a graphic designer at the office, on a new campaign for Brightside, and so far, she hasn't been giving me what I want, so I'm scouring the internet for examples of what I'm aiming for.

The Mammoths are down by two goals at the start of the third period, and though Dane isn't letting it show, I can tell from his expression that he's frustrated. It has to be hard to watch his team play while he's stuck up here, even if it is his own fault.

I'm writing an email when a text comes into my phone.

Dane: Still mad at me?

I shoot him a glare and don't respond. My phone immediately buzzes with another text and I want to ignore it, but I can't. My brow furrows when I see the new message isn't from Dane, but from the designer I've been working with.

Julie: I'm sorry I'm texting so late, I've been busy with my kids all evening. I just hopped on my email and saw your messages. Jane told me at the end of the workday that Monica has the Brightside account now.

I read the message twice, not believing it. My blood pressure is rising steadily when I text Jane.

Josie: Did you give Monica my Brightside account?

Jane: The client belongs to my agency, and yes. You aren't available for in-person meetings right now and Monica is.

I want to throw my phone at the wall. Why did my aunt give me this damn job babysitting Dane? It isn't adding anything to my PR skill set, and it just cost me my biggest client.

Of course she gave it to Monica. Of all my coworkers, I dislike her the most.

Dane: What's wrong? Did the bookstore run out of books?

Josie: Eat shit.

Dane: We're going out with some of the guys after the game, you need a drink or three.

I wish I could walk away. From this suite, from

watching over Dane *and* from my job. I'm too broke for that, though.

After closing my laptop, I take a paperback out of my bag and open it. Meeting Dane's gaze across the room, I scratch my cheek with my middle finger, the same move he used on Arnold the day we met.

A smile tugs on his lips as he looks away.

He's mostly gotten my nice, diplomatic side up until now. It's time for Dane to meet unfiltered, zero-fucks-given Josie.

"AND SHE HEATS UP LEFTOVER FISH AND BROCCOLI IN the office microwave at least once a week, which is actually worse than when she opens a can of sardines at her desk. Who does that?"

Lucas nods and gives me a sympathetic look. We've been at a bar for nearly an hour with other Mammoths players. Chicago won the game 4–1, and even though tomorrow morning we head out early for another road trip, lots of guys are drinking away their sorrows over the loss.

I'm three margaritas in, complaining to Lucas about Monica while watching Dane out of the corner of my eye and daring him to misbehave.

He's at the table next to mine with three teammates, several women swarming around them like flies on shit.

"I swear Dalton saves his shits for the team plane," Lucas says. "He could go at his hotel, but he likes to take a big shit as soon as we get on the plane and then we all have to smell it for the whole flight."

"Inconsiderate," I say, shaking my head and sipping my drink. "Just like Monica. I spilled soup on my shirt at work once and she was like, 'Oh, I'd let you borrow one I have in my office, but it's too small for you.' Like, why say that? Just say nothing."

One of the women at Dane's table cozies up to his side, trying to look casual as her body molds against his. He's been nursing his drinks, only on his second beer of the night.

"Do you ever get time off?" Lucas asks me. "Days when you don't have to keep track of Dane?"

"No."

"Can you get someone to cover for you for an evening sometime?"

I scoff. "I'd love to, but there's no one."

"I could talk to him. See if he'd agree to stay in for an evening."

Lucas doesn't know Dane very well. He didn't

listen to his coach and team owner telling him to behave. Why would he listen to a teammate?

"Good luck with that," I say. "He lies."

"Well, how can I get you alone?" Lucas asks.

He leans in so close I can smell his soap and cologne. My head is swimming from the alcohol, but even with my judgment impaired, I know I can't get involved with one of Dane's teammates. I have to keep my focus on this assignment because I need that promotion. I have student loans to pay off, and somehow, I have to buy another car.

Dane is laughing, tipping his bottle of beer to his lips as he glances over at us. His happy expression fades, turning serious.

He sets the beer down and says something to the woman superglued to him. She moves away and he gets up, walking toward the bar's front door.

"I have to go," I tell Lucas, grabbing my bag and following Dane.

"Dane," I call as he walks. "Dane, stop!"

He turns to face me, his gaze dark and angry. "What? You need a condom? Looks like you and Lucas are about to fuck right here in front of everyone."

I recoil, taken aback by his hostility.

"What are you talking about? We never even

touched, and that blond just had to peel her body off yours so you could get up."

"I didn't encourage her."

"And I didn't encourage Lucas. I need to pay for my drinks before we go."

"I already paid for them."

"Oh. Thanks."

He exhales through his nose. "You're not a puck bunny, Josie. Don't let Lucas make you into one."

I give him a confused look. "Dane, I was just talking to him. A shitty work thing happened today and I was talking to him about that."

"Why can't you talk to me about it?"

I laugh, getting so lightheaded I reach for a nearby table to steady myself. "You mean besides the fact that you don't care?"

He puts an arm around my waist, the heat of his solid body against mine making me gasp.

"Let's get you to the car," he says.

"I'm fine."

"Stop arguing and let me get you to the car."

"Stop helping and let me argue," I say, knowing it doesn't even make sense.

He walks me out to his Range Rover, helping me into the passenger seat. I lean my head back against the seat, wishing I wouldn't have had three strong drinks when we have to fly out so early tomorrow.

"I feel like we're even," Dane says as he gets into the driver's seat.

"Oh, really?"

"Yeah, I got wasted last night and you got wasted tonight. Even."

I laugh at his flawed logic. "I'm not wasted."

"You're not sober."

"That's the truth. If you bolt on me right now, I don't think I could catch you."

His smile is wry. "I hate to break it to you, but there's no chance you could ever catch me in a race unless I wanted you to."

"Hey, I played volleyball in middle school."

His deep, full-throated laugh makes me warm all over. "Can't compete with that, Nosy. You're a fucking boss."

I turn up the air conditioning, swearing to stick to one drink only when we go out in the future. Or even better, none.

"You can talk to me, you know," Dane says.

"I talk to you all the time."

"No, I mean back at the bar when you said you talked to Lucas because I don't care. That's not true."

I close my eyes, wishing everything would stop spinning. "I lost my biggest account at work today."

"What happened?"

Usually, I protect Jane. I don't know if it's because of the alcohol or because she took away my client and didn't even have the courtesy to tell me, but I don't feel like making her sound better than she is.

"My boss is also my aunt. She's my dad's sister and she always hated my mom before my mom died, so she treats me like shit. She took it away because she could. Just like I'm here working twenty-four seven on a job no one else wants."

"I'm sorry."

My laugh is bitter. "The worst part is that I still want her approval so badly. I hardly have any family left. So I try like a fucking idiot to make her proud of me."

"You're not a fucking idiot."

"Sometimes I am."

"Karma will catch up with her."

I scoff. "Bullshit. If karma was a thing, my car wouldn't have been repossessed. My mom wouldn't have died."

"Hey--"

I cut him off. "I don't want to talk anymore."

After pausing for a couple of seconds, he says, "Okay."

He doesn't say anything else. We get back to his place and I go straight to my bedroom to curl up with Mr. Darcy.

There's a one-hundred-percent chance I'm going to be miserably ill and hungover on the flight. I fall asleep in my clothes, needing to catch five hours of sleep before we have to leave for the airport.

fourteen

JOSIE

"Hey, I've been thinking."

I just woke up and wiped away my drool, and instead of responding to Dane, I squint at him.

"How long was I asleep?"

"The whole flight. We're descending."

"Wow."

I sit up straight, my neck protesting after being in a weird position for a long time. Dane asked the team doctor to give me something for my air sickness before we boarded the plane, and whatever he gave me did the trick.

"I didn't get sick at all."

I can hardly believe it. Instead of puking into a bag and feeling like death, I slept. I actually feel pretty decent. My hangover headache is even gone.

"What was in that drink you gave me this morning?" I ask Dane.

"That was my juju juice. I can't disclose the recipe, but it kicks the shit out of hangovers every time."

He does a ninja karate chop with his hands and nods.

"Juju juice," I say, glad I drank it without question.

I glance over at him, wondering if I should give up on trying to figure him out. He can be a dick, but he can also be thoughtful.

"Anyway, back to my idea," he says. "You should quit your job."

I clear my throat and look around, still not feeling completely awake.

"Can I get some water?"

"Yeah, we'll get you some water," he says impatiently. "But did you hear me? You need to quit your job."

I live paycheck to paycheck on my salary. A seven-figure earner like him just doesn't get what it means to struggle.

"I can't do that."

"Yeah, you can. Just call your aunt and tell her to shove it up her ass."

I glare at him. "That way you can get rid of me and I can live in a van down by the river?"

His jaw drops an inch. "You watch *SNL*?"

"Of course."

He lowers his brows, looking skeptical. "Favorite skit ever?"

I consider, because that's like asking a mother to choose her favorite child.

"I can narrow it down to 'Schweddy Balls,' 'Dick in a Box' and 'Debbie Downer.' Don't ask me to choose between the three."

His brows lower even farther. "What about 'More Cowbell'? 'Wayne's World'?"

"'Wayne's World' is in my top five. I'm not a big fan of 'More Cowbell.'"

He arches his brows and puts his palms out in mock surrender. "Clearly you haven't watched it enough times. I'll have the videographer put it on a loop for you to watch on our next flight."

"Sounds like an excellent use of her time."

He laughs a single note and nudges my shoulder with his. "Last season, she made a looped video with a clip of Dalton tripping and falling while we were all walking through the tunnel at our arena. One of his hands landed on a dude's crotch and they were both mortified. We watched it on the DVD players on our buses for the rest of the season."

"Such a fine example to kids."

He scoffs. "No one outside of the team ever knew about it, relax. It's funny as shit. I'll show it to you sometime."

Our plane touches down and I grip the armrests out of habit. Dane grins at me.

"You know the seat belt will keep you in your seat, right? You don't actually have to hold yourself in with your hands."

"Eat shit, I'm a nervous flier."

"Didn't the medicine help with that?"

I turn to him, alarmed. "What did you have the doctor give me?"

"I didn't ask him to give you anything. I'm not a fucking doctor. He just said he'd give you something to take the edge off your anxiety and settle your stomach."

I exhale, reminding myself that we're on the ground and I did have a much better flight than usual.

"Sorry."

"Hey, about you quitting your job," he says.

"I can't quit my job, dickface. I need the money."

"You call all your clients dickfaces?"

"Only the one who's a dickface."

He groans with frustration. "Anyway. You should quit and start your own company. I can help."

I shake my head and laugh at the suggestion. "Oh, really? And how would you do that?"

He shrugs. "I have some ideas. Let's talk about it after the game."

I try to remember if we're flying out immediately after the game, and I realize I don't even know where we are.

"What city are we in?"

"Nashville. We can't fly out until tomorrow morning because they couldn't coordinate the planes to get us out tonight."

The seat belt lights go off and I unfasten mine. I remember the deadline for the Brightside presentation, and it hits me all over again that I've lost the account.

I've considered sending résumés out to other PR companies a few times, but I've never been able to bring myself to do it. I tell myself Jane is the hardest on me because she knows I can take it. That it's tough love to help me succeed no matter what comes my way.

This doesn't feel like that, though. This feels like a knife in my back. I worked at the agency for years before getting my first big solo account with Brightside. And she took it away without even telling me.

I'm caught between a rock and a hard place. I want something better for myself, but I can't afford to miss a single paycheck. I might as well check job listing sites while I'm at the hotel and arena today, now that I don't have any other work to do besides watching over Dane.

DANE'S FIRST GAME BACK AFTER HIS SUSPENSION IS A 5–2 victory. By the time he walks out of the locker room, freshly showered and wearing a suit, it's nearly eleven p.m. and I'm tired.

"Hey, are you guys coming out?" Lucas asks, following behind Dane.

"Nah, not tonight."

Lucas looks agitated. "Come on, man. Come out." He glances at me.

"No," Dane says, and I'm relieved.

I rarely drink, and last night, I made a fool of myself. I'm looking forward to some food, a shower and a great night of sleep.

Lucas walks over to me. He's good-looking and nice, someone I'd normally be drawn to.

"You can still come if you want to," he says.

"Where he goes, I go." I shrug.

Lucas glares at Dane. "Can you keep from being a drunken asshole for one night so she can have some time off her twenty-four seven job?"

Dane narrows his eyes and a prickle of awareness tingles on my skin. Fresh off his suspension, I don't want him fighting with a teammate with reporters swarming all over.

"I appreciate the invitation, but I'm going to stay with Dane," I say.

A smile tugs on Dane's lips as he puts an arm around my shoulder.

"Knock it off," I say, shrugging his arm off and scowling. "I'm not a hydrant for you to piss all over."

"You're a fucking toddler," Lucas says to Dane. "I'll see you around, Josie."

"You ready?" Dane asks me.

"Yeah."

"I'm doing you a favor," he says as we walk out to the car that will take us to the hotel. "Lucas is nice and all, but he's not the guy for you."

"Oh? And how do you know that?"

"Because I know him. He's too emotional."

I laugh at his reasoning. "Meaning what?"

"When his last girlfriend cheated on him, he was a mess for like two months. He doesn't know how to button it up and move on."

"So he's not a manwhore like you? That makes me like him more."

He furrows his brow. "Just because I don't like committed relationships, that doesn't make me a manwhore. I've never promised a woman more than I was willing to give."

"So you're up front about it? You tell them it's only going to be one night?"

He shrugs. "If it comes up, which it usually doesn't."

"And then what? The next morning, they try to give you their number and you say no thanks?"

"I try to avoid that conversation by not being around the next morning."

I cringe. "Look up manwhore in the dictionary sometime."

We find the dark SUV with the driver taking us

to our hotel, both of us getting in the back of the vehicle.

"So anyway," Dane says. "I think you should start your own company."

I get a good, long laugh out of that suggestion. "I'm a junior publicist without any experience running a business. Once I pay my bills next week I'll have about eighty bucks to my name."

"I could help seed you with money."

My stomach rolls at the idea. "Absolutely not. I can't afford to owe anyone money."

"Look, you've got a niche thing going here. Watching over pro athletes. I'll become a model player and say it's all because of you. Then, you hire more people to do this job for other athletes, actors and musicians. It's a gold mine."

I can't believe he thought of this. It's not a bad idea at all, but I'm too risk-averse to try it.

"Maybe," I say, knowing if I tell him no, it'll cause an argument.

"The number one rule my agent taught me is to know your own value. You're undervaluing yourself in a big way, and your aunt is taking advantage of it."

It hurts to hear someone say that about one of

the few family members I have left, even though he's probably right.

"I'll think about it, okay?"

He nods, typing into his phone. "I'm ordering Chinese delivery to our room. What do you want?"

I haven't eaten anything but half of a sub sandwich at lunchtime and I'm ravenous.

"Veggie fried rice, crab Rangoon and an egg roll."

He grins at me. "Is that all?"

"That's all."

Our driver drops us off at the door of our hotel and we go up to our fourth-floor room. The hotel staff left a gift basket on the desk with fruit, champagne, bottled water and snacks. I shake my head as I open it and take out a bag of chips.

"What?" Dane asks.

"At the hotels I stay in, you have to pay if you open the bottled water. And there are loud wall air conditioners and sketchy carpet stains."

"Think about my idea," he says. "You have nothing to lose."

He's partially right—I have nothing. Nothing to invest. No experience hiring, budgeting or recruiting new clients. I wish I could take his advice, but it would most likely put me in a deeper hole than the one I already live in.

"I'm getting in the shower," I say, gathering toiletries and clothing from my bag.

Dane's on his bed looking at his phone, his suit jacket hanging over the chair at the desk.

"Hey, put on those little black shorts and a tank top," he says, not looking up from the screen.

My heart pounds erratically. "What?"

He meets my gaze. "You know what I said."

"Yeah, but why?"

"Because you look hot in them. You've got a nice ass."

My jaw falls and I force it closed. "I'm not here for your entertainment."

He hums in amusement, his gaze back on his phone screen. "You like that I think you're hot, Josie. Wear the shorts."

I want to argue, but he's right. I've always been the bookworm. The sidekick to the girls most guys wanted. It feels good to know Dane thinks I'm attractive, superficial as that may be.

"If I wear them, it'll be because they're comfortable, not because you like my ass in them."

"Bullshit. You'd like nothing more than to lie across my lap and get that gorgeous ass spanked."

I keep my head down as I rush to the bathroom, my clothes clutched to my chest to hide my nipples. No man has ever said anything like that to me. My heart is racing and I'm hot all over.

I won't admit to him that he's right because I can't even process how right he is. I didn't think I'd be turned on by spanking, but when Dane suggested it just now?

It turned me on hard.

fifteen

DANE

I push a button on the screen of the treadmill in the team training room, increasing the speed. Sweat rolls down my chest. When I swipe the back of my hand over my forehead, droplets of sweat go flying. I kick the speed up as high as I can manage for the next three minutes.

HIIT training is good for endurance, and it also helps calm my mind when I'm restless.

I can't stop thinking about Josie. Though I can't pinpoint exactly when it happened, I've gotten used to having her around. More than used to it, actually.

I *like* having her around. That's something I've never experienced. Usually, once I've spent the night with a woman, there's nothing more to talk about. No reason to see her.

Josie is funny, though. Interesting. Smart. My physical attraction to her started *after* I got to know her better. That's another first.

My so-called date with Abigail Matthews is just a few days away. We're meeting up for lunch on the day of a game in Chicago. The only bright side is that I haven't forgotten Josie's offer to "coach" me on a suitable date.

I'm going to have some fun with that.

"WHAT'S THIS ABOUT?" JOSIE ASKS ME AFTER THE game that night. "Am I dressed up enough?"

I just showered and dressed in a dark suit with a white dress shirt and a blue tie. I pretend to think about her question, studying her from head to toe.

When I texted her earlier and told her to dress up for our after-game plans tonight, she took me seriously. She's wearing a red dress cut to show off her cleavage perfectly. It falls just past her knees, so I take in her shapely calves before I get to her nude low-cut heels. Her black wrap covers her arms and all I can think about is tugging on it and throwing it aside.

Hopefully later.

"You're dressed perfectly," I say, offering her my arm.

She wrinkles her nose in confusion. "You didn't answer my first question."

"I'll tell you in just a minute."

I tilt my head in the direction of the exit, and we walk toward it.

"This better not be about my job," she says in a low tone that carries a note of panic. "Please tell me you aren't trying to get me a different job. Or to start my own company. I'm not ready for that."

A few people have glanced at us, and I don't want to say anything about our plans with anyone else in earshot, so I just shrug.

"You'd be great at it," I say.

"Where are we going?" she demands, stopping. "If I'm walking into some business pitch session, a) I'm going to put hair remover on your head while you're sleeping tonight, and b) I need to prepare myself. Which I literally cannot do if I haven't had any notice."

"It's nothing like that."

She gives me a skeptical look. "I'm not a charity case. If I wanted your help starting a business, I'd ask for it."

Now I'm getting irritated. There's a car waiting outside and I'm going to tell her where we're going as soon as I know no one can hear us talking.

"For fuck's sake, Josie. I just played twenty-five minutes and I'm starving. Can we go?"

She keeps walking, her eyes narrowed slightly as she looks up at me.

"Good game, by the way," she says.

"Thanks."

We won 3–1. I got a pregame boost when I heard the news that Sam Styles broke his ankle when he took a bad fall shooting hoops with teammates.

That bastard deserves two broken ankles and lifelong impotence. He and my ex are equally responsible for what went down between the two of them, but he's the only one whose ass I can beat.

As soon as we reach the end of the hallway and walk through the double doors toward the player exit, I tell Josie what's going on.

"We're going on a practice date."

"A practice date?"

"Yep. You told Tamara from PR that you'd

coach me before my lunch with what's her name from TikTok."

"Abigail," she says wryly. "Her name is Abigail."

Damn, she looks hot in that dress. Her eye makeup is slightly darker than usual and she's holding her chin just a little higher. I hope it's because that dress makes her feel confident. She sure as fuck should feel that way.

"You ready for this, Coach?" I ask her with a grin.

She laughs lightly. "You're telling me I have one night to make you into a perfect gentleman?"

"Something like that."

Her teeth sink into her lower lip as she gives me a sexy smile. An invisible current passes between us. She makes me want to be anything but a perfect gentleman, but I also want her to know she's special. Not just another random lay.

"Okay, first tip," she says. "Start out the date with a sincere compliment."

"You take my breath away in that dress."

I didn't even have to consider what to say. There are a hundred compliments on the tip of my tongue. And the shine in her eyes right now makes me want to say all of them.

"Thank you," she says, slightly breathless.

Breathless is good. Breathless is very, very good.

I offer her my arm again. "We have a reservation. Are you ready to go?"

She nods and takes my arm. Operation Practice Date is underway.

"Movies were our thing," Josie says a couple of hours later. "And *SNL*. She introduced me to *SNL*."

We finished our steaks and sides an hour ago, but we're still sitting in a downtown Nashville steak house, a curtain hiding our private booth from onlookers. It's going on one a.m., but as Josie tells me about her mom, I don't feel remotely tired.

"What were some of her favorite skits?" I ask.

"She loved Chris Farley and Mike Myers. I think 'Van Down by the River' was her all-time favorite."

"Did you guys watch movies at home or at the theater?"

"Usually at home. But if there was a big movie coming out, we'd go see it on Friday night. Always with a huge bucket of popcorn and Cherry Cokes."

"My mom always loved movie popcorn, too," I say, smiling as I think about her.

"Is she gone? If you don't mind me asking?"

"You can ask me anything. She's still around. My parents live in Naples, Florida. Dad's a financial planner and Mom does interior design, but just for fun."

"Isn't it funny how even as an adult, you see people with their moms and just long for your own? I'd give anything to make cookies with her or go for a walk with her. To hear her voice again and see her smile...it would be everything to me."

She clears her throat and looks away. I reach across the table and take her hand gently in mine.

"Just checking in," our server says, opening the curtain slightly. "Anything you guys need?"

"No, I think we're good," I say.

"Okay, great."

We had drinks and dinner, split a piece of raspberry cheesecake and I already paid the bill. If the magic of our time together will be over when we leave this curtained booth, though, I don't want to go.

Josie stifles a yawn and smiles sheepishly.

"I guess we should go," I say.

"Yeah, we have to get up at four thirty."

She gets her wrap and bag and slides out of the booth, and I follow. I fight my urge to cup her cheek and kiss her. This is the moment. If I'd asked her on a real date, I'd kiss her here and take her back to the hotel, where we'd do a lot more than kiss until it's time to leave for our flight.

This night has been very real to me, but I don't know if she's ready for more yet.

"You did great," she says over her shoulder as she moves the curtain aside.

"We're not done yet."

I wink at her and she smiles. It's scary how hooked I am on that smile. And her laugh creates an actual, physical warmth in my chest.

What the hell is happening to me? Is it just that I haven't had sex in what feels like a lifetime?

Our hotel is close to the restaurant. The driver drops us off at the front door and I put my hand on Josie's lower back as we walk inside.

"I had fun tonight," I say.

"Me too."

We have to share the elevator with a man in a rumpled suit, so I don't get her alone again until we're walking to our room. When we get there, we face each other.

"So," she says softly.

"So."

"This is where, if you like her and want to go out again, you kiss her."

"How do I know if she likes me back?"

She holds my gaze, opening her mouth and then closing it before she finally speaks. "You'll know."

"I guess if she didn't like me, she'd try to rush inside," I say softly. "She wouldn't look at me like she's waiting for something."

Josie swallows, breathing a little faster now. "Exactly."

I reach up and cup her cheek. Her skin is soft and warm. She leans into my touch and her eyes flutter closed.

"Dane..."

"Josie."

She opens her eyes again and says, "We can't."

"No?"

She shakes her head and I deflate. I won't ask her to explain or try to change her mind, because I only want her if she wants me just as much.

I take out the key card and open the door, Josie going straight into the bathroom. She emerges ten minutes later in boxers and a T-shirt, her makeup off.

"Good night," she says stiffly, climbing under the covers.

"Night."

She turns her back to me, the last of tonight's magic disappearing.

sixteen

JOSIE

"I HEAR YOU'RE OFFICIALLY ONE OF US," JENN SAYS from the other side of our table at a downtown Mexican restaurant.

I furrow my brow. "Not sure what you mean."

Elena laughs from beside me. "Did you and Dane really think you could sneak out like that, all dressed up and looking like you were about thirty seconds from ripping each other's clothes off, and no one would notice?"

Oh. Our practice date the other night. My face heats as it sets in that we're the object of team gossip now. If this somehow gets back to my aunt, I can kiss that promotion goodbye.

"It wasn't what it looked like," I assure Jenn and Elena.

Jenn raises her empty glass as our server walks past our table. "Hey, can we get another round?"

I groan. The margaritas here are so big that I'm lightheaded from the first one I finished. And the more I drink, the more likely I am to spill my guts about how I really feel about Dane.

"It was a practice date," I tell my new friends. "He's going out with a med student when we're in Chicago next. She hit him up on social media and I think it'll be good for his image."

Elana shakes her head, looking amused. "There's so much to unpack there."

I'm enjoying our afternoon together so much that I'm likely to tell them anything they want to know. Aiden is hosting a cookout for the team, but it's players only, so Jenn and Elena asked me if I wanted to window-shop and have lunch. I jumped at the chance for some girl time.

"Whose idea was this practice date?" Jenn asks, air-quoting *practice date*.

I pinch my brows together, trying to remember. "I think his."

"And the practice part is...what? Because Dane doesn't know how to go out on a date?"

I take a sip from the fresh margarita that was just delivered, trying to figure out how to diplomatically answer that.

"Well, it won't be good for his image if he asks her which hole she wants it in thirty seconds into the date," I say, shrugging.

"If she's trolling athletes online, she's hoping he'll bring two teammates and fill all her holes at once," Elena cracks.

Jenn has already drained a third of the second margarita. She's flushed and full of smiles.

"I can't wait any longer to ask," she says. "Did you guys *practice* sleeping together?"

I cringe. "God, no. Nothing like that."

Elena looks like she's about to burst with excitement. She grins and gently smacks the table. "This is the tension part. I read lots of romance novels. Dane has to pretend he doesn't want her and she pretends she doesn't want him, but they're secretly sneaking looks at each other and coming up with things like practice dates as excuses to be together."

I laugh. "I mean...have there been moments of

attraction? Yes. But Dane and I would drive each other crazy."

"How are you pretending you're not crazy with jealousy over him taking another woman out on a date?"

I take a break to eat chips and salsa, hoping one of them will bring up another subject, but they turn into the two most patient people ever, just waiting for me to stop eating and answer the question.

"I told you, it's not like that with us."

Elena scoffs. "It is, though. Aaron said you two spend every second together."

"We kind of have to, I'm his glorified babysitter."

"Aiden said Dane's pissed about Lucas paying so much attention to you."

I shake my head and laugh. "Your husbands sound like gossipy teenage girls."

"That's how it is on a team," Jenn says. "Everyone knows everyone's business."

"Deep down, Dane's a really good guy," Elena says. "It hurt him really badly when his wife cheated. He acts cynical now, but I don't think he really is."

"Do you guys know anything about what

happened with his ex-wife?" I ask. "How did he find out about it?"

Jenn's shoulders sink. "He walked in on them. He was out of town and his trip got cut short, so he wanted to surprise her and come home early. He had flowers for her in his hand when he found them going at it in his own bed."

I close my eyes, imagining how hard that must have been for him.

"He and Sam had a huge fight then and there," Jenn says. "Sam ended up running out of the house naked, with blood running down his face."

"If he played for another team, how did he know Dane's..." For some reason, I can't call her his wife. "His, um...ex."

Jenn lets Elena take that one.

"Dane and Sam used to be teammates."

I bury my face in my hands, then sigh heavily and look at Elena. "Poor Dane."

"Yeah. Now you know why everyone's so happy he's into you. There hasn't been anyone serious since Cruella."

I arch a brow, amused. "Cruella?"

"It's what we call his ex," Jenn says. "She's tall and villainous, so it fits."

Our food arrives and I take the opportunity to change the subject.

"Catch me up on what's happening with you guys," I say. "Let me live vicariously through you."

Elena laughs. "Well, I've changed a whole lot of diapers and prepped a whole lot of baby food in the past couple of weeks. It's exciting."

"Beats following a hockey player all over the country," I say.

"Ugh." Jenn rolls her eyes. "I'd travel with Aiden if I could. It gets old going to bed alone. No vibrator compares to him."

"I used to think that, too," Elena says. "Now I just enjoy the extra sleep."

"We need all the details on the practice date," Jenn says, back on the subject of me and Dane.

I can't get out of it, so I answer every question they ask me. I leave out the part about our almost-kiss though, because I still haven't sorted out my feelings on it.

I wanted him to kiss me. I know it's a terrible idea and will likely end with me getting hurt, but the one thing I'm not at all confused about is that I'm very attracted to Dane.

And now that I know he's attracted to me, too,

the only thing keeping us apart is my fading willpower.

"There she is!" Dane cries when I walk into Jenn and Aiden's house a few hours later. "My bodyguard's here to carry me home."

He's trashed. I can tell from his slurred words and the way he's about to fall off the barstool he's sitting on.

"We got in the hot tub," he says merrily. "There were no hot chicks in there, just a bunch of dudes. Zero stars, do not recommend."

I quit drinking halfway through my second drink, and we shopped for a couple of hours before taking an Uber home, so I'm completely sober.

"Are you ready to go home?" I ask him.

"Hell no!" Aiden walks over and puts an arm around Dane. "The party's just getting started!"

It's cool outside, but Jenn and Aiden have outdoor heaters on their patio. A few guys are still in the oversized hot tub.

"Put on your suit," Dane says to me. "I want to get in the hot tub with a hot chick."

"I don't have a swimsuit."

"You can borrow mine," he offers, sliding off the barstool and stumbling.

Lucas puts an arm out to stabilize him and Dane scowls.

"I'm fine," he says sharply. "Just need to get these off."

He starts to pull down his swim trunks and I rush forward to stop him, trying to pull the waistband back up.

"Oh, you want to do this right here?" He grins.

"Pull your trunks back up."

"I'm gonna...borrow 'em to you."

I meet Jenn's gaze across the patio. "Is there somewhere he can lie down for a little bit?"

"Yeah, use one of the guest rooms upstairs. Any of them you want."

Dane laughs into my neck, putting his arms around me and letting me pull his trunks up all the way. "Is it nap time? Can I take a nap on top of you? Naked while thrusting my hips?"

"Aaron just threw up in a bush," someone says. "Can someone help me carry him to the couch?"

"Let's go," I tell Dane, putting an arm around his waist to help him walk.

"It's naked nap time!" he yells, pumping his fist.

Aaron is arguing with the teammates who are

trying to help him to a couch. At least Dane is a happy drunk and not a belligerent one. It looks like the teammates hit the whiskey pretty hard this afternoon.

I manage to get Dane up to a guest room, where he lies facedown on the white quilt covering a king-size bed.

"Don't violate my ass, Nosy," he mumbles.

Shaking my head, I go to the bathroom. When I return, he's out cold, snoring hard. I lie down next to him and get out my phone.

Everyone out back probably thinks we're screwing, but I'm playing a crossword game while Dane sleeps it off. The truth doesn't keep the rumor mill churning, though.

seventeen

DANE

I OPEN MY EYES AND THEN CLOSE THEM AGAIN, A faint headache making me groan.

"Drink this." Josie passes me something.

Leaning on my elbow, I take the bottle of water, open it and chug half of it. There's not much light in the unfamiliar room.

"Where are we?"

"Aiden and Jenn's guest room."

Right. Whiskey. Hot tub. More whiskey. I remember everything now, including asking Josie for a naked nap.

She's reading something on her phone. I drink the rest of the water and turn to face her.

"I told you not to violate my ass." I'm half-sorry and half-amused.

"I somehow fought off the temptation," she deadpans.

"How was your girl time?"

She sets down her phone and turns onto her side to face me. "It was good."

"How long was I out?"

"Four hours. It's after eight."

I take her hand in mine, her eyes widening as I stroke my thumb over her smooth skin.

"You're beautiful," I say.

She smiles. "You need to keep sleeping it off, Foster."

"I'm sober. And you're beautiful. Your eyes are the prettiest green; they're like moss. And you have a cute little nose and a smile that takes my breath away."

"This is how you do it, isn't it?"

"Do what?"

"Charm women even though you're an annoying asshole."

Her tone is light and I know what she's really

doing—trying to deflect my compliments. She's self-deprecating, always turning compliments into jokes.

I won't stop until she acknowledges what I'm saying, even if I have to compliment every part of her until I reach her cuticles.

"You even make pajama shorts look sexy with those legs and that ass."

She scoffs. "Are you buttering me up because you have bad news? You might as well just come out with it."

I gently brush the hair away from her face. "I snuck a picture of you during our practice date. You were talking to our server. I look at it so much I've got it memorized. Your pretty pink lips and your neck drive me fucking crazy. Your hair was over your shoulder and I wanted to kiss your neck so badly, you have no idea. I could see almost half of your breasts in that dress."

Her eyes are locked onto mine. She gives my hand the tiniest little squeeze.

"I'm not letting Lucas lay a hand on you," I say.

"Is celibacy part of my job description now?" she asks, her voice barely more than a whisper.

"Until you realize how much you want me it is."

Her lips curve up in a small smile. "You do

realize you're going on a date with another woman tomorrow in Chicago."

"Only because you want me to."

"Have you seen pictures of her? You may end up liking her."

Aggravation flares in my chest. Why can't she just acknowledge there's something between us? I don't totally understand what it is, but I know I want to fuck her and get the hell away from her as quickly as possible at the same time.

"I already like someone else. And you should see her. She's got this hot, curvy body that makes me insane."

I put my hand on her hip, my thumb brushing over the skin exposed by her shirt riding up slightly. Her lips part and her brows pinch together with concern.

"What's there to be worried about right now, Nosy?"

She moves my hand away and tugs her shirt down. "You're used to playing with people. Women are expendable to you. You don't get it. If you and I got involved, you'd be tired of me in what, three weeks? If that? I'd just be one of many notches in your bedpost, and I'd be fired from my job over it."

I hate that she thinks so little of me. I haven't

even looked at other women since meeting her, and still she doesn't believe my interest in her is sincere.

"What have I done to make you feel like you'd be a notch on a bedpost?"

She sighs softly. "The whole reason I'm here is because you can't control yourself. Whether it's alcohol or women, you just...go overboard."

"It's not that I can't control myself; it's that I've chosen not to. I work hard and don't see why I shouldn't get to play hard, too."

I can tell she's suppressing an eye roll. "Your *playing* is what landed you a full-time babysitter, Dane."

"A hot babysitter. I'm not mad about it."

She laughs lightly. "You don't know when to quit, do you?"

"Never. When I want something, I never quit."

I run the backs of my fingers over her jawline, the only touch she seems comfortable with. Even though I've spent more time with her than I've ever spent with a woman, I never get tired of her.

"We should go back downstairs," she says softly.

"We should stay here."

She sits up in bed. My disappointment is strong and immediate. I know she's attracted to me, but she won't give in to it.

"So you won't sleep with me," I say, a wave of dizziness hitting when I sit up.

"Accurate. I haven't changed my mind in the last two and a half minutes."

"But you're okay being in bed with me for several hours? What's the difference?"

She stands up, walks over to switch on the light, and puts her shoes on. "I think you know the difference between being side by side in bed fully clothed and full sex, Dane. And if not, I don't get paid enough to explain it to you."

I smile at her as I get out of bed, my headache duller than it was when I woke up but still there. Her sense of humor is one of my favorite things about her.

"I guess what I'm saying is, what's the difference between everyone thinking we're sleeping together and actually doing it?"

Her gaze locks onto mine. "The difference is here." She puts a hand on her heart. "I can't just sleep with someone and not have feelings for them. I couldn't do my job anymore if we were involved. It would be too complicated. Not for you, for me."

I nod, her admission sobering me all the way up. I want her so badly I can hardly stand it, but I don't want to hurt her. She's right—I'm not a relationship guy. She deserves much better than me.

She puts a hand on the doorknob, ready to leave. I walk over, putting a palm on the door to hold it closed. Her hair is rumpled from lying down and it looks sexy as hell. I realize it's not any one quality about her that drives me crazy with desire; it's everything.

"I'm still not letting Lucas lay a hand on you," I say.

A smile plays on her lips. "Maybe I should decide who puts their hands on me."

I shake my head, my jaw flexing with annoyance. "Not if it's him."

"Why not?"

I sigh heavily, aggravated. "Why are you pushing this? If it would be unprofessional to sleep with me, wouldn't it be unprofessional to sleep with one of my teammates?"

She shrugs. "I'm only doing this job for a couple more months at the most."

I scoff, narrowing my eyes. "Lucas will have to walk over my cold, rotting corpse to get to you, no matter when it is."

I've had nightmares about walking in on the two

of them going at it, Josie screaming his name. Every time I wake up covered in sweat, my heart racing.

"Why do you hate him so much?"

I lean in so close I can smell the light floral perfume she wears on her neck. It's all I can do not to grab her and kiss her. I know I don't deserve her, but my body doesn't care.

"I don't hate him at all. The same goes for any of my other teammates."

Her brows shoot up in surprise and she swallows hard.

"Why?"

"Because if I can't have you, they sure as fuck can't."

I lean back, moving my hand away from the door. Her hand looks shaky as she turns the handle.

I won't cross the line with her, but I can't help myself from getting close enough to make us both wonder if I will.

eighteen

JOSIE

"I can cancel," Dane says.

I shake my head, pretending I don't care. "Have lunch with the girl. You need to eat anyway."

"You should come with me."

I laugh lightly, reaching up to fix the collar on the navy polo shirt he's wearing. "You'd love that, wouldn't you? A date with two women?"

His expression remains serious. I think we may have reached the point where Dane knows when I'm lying. Or at least bypassing the real issue entirely.

A perfunctory date with a fan seemed like a good idea when I came up with it. And now, I hate it. Even though my feelings for Dane are all over the place, the thought of him on a date with another woman makes me want to crawl into bed and cry.

"It's just a quick lunch," he says. "Sandwiches at a deli. Then I'll head back to the arena."

"Yeah, I know."

We're in our hotel room, which doesn't help. Traveling everywhere with Dane and sharing hotel rooms with him means we've gotten close. We can read each other well. Whether sexually involved or not, we woke up in the same room this morning and went down to breakfast together. He went to the arena after that for pregame stuff with his team while I worked in the hotel lounge.

I've been thinking about what Dane said, though I haven't said a word about it to anyone. Maybe someday I could start my own business. Since I have lots of time on my hands, I'm working on a business plan.

Though I'm trying not to think jealous thoughts, I feel stabby over how good Dane smells right now. The pine scent of his body wash wafted out of the bathroom with him after he showered.

"You could have used the soap the hotel provides," I mutter.

He knits his brows together. "What?"

"Nothing."

I busy myself organizing my toiletry bag, wishing I hadn't said anything. His little hum of amusement makes me cringe.

"Are you saying I smell good?"

His tone annoys the crap out of me. Dane can't just take a compliment; he has to toy with it. Dangle it. Stretch it out until I'm practically feral with annoyance.

He walks over and stands next to me, his closeness making me warm from head to toe. Still, I refuse to acknowledge him. I am entirely focused on making sure my eye makeup remover container is tightly closed.

"Hey," he says softly.

I turn and look up at him, my heart racing. Why does he have to be so impossibly good-looking?

"I can cancel."

I shake my head, not trusting my voice. He slowly runs the tip of his index finger over my jawline, from my ear to my chin.

"I'd rather stay here with you," he says.

Tension crackles in the air between us. If he

stays, there's no doubt what will happen. I'm slowly losing my will to stay professional and not get my heart broken. It's been so long since I've felt anything for a man, and I've never felt anything on the scale of what I feel for Dane. Even if I know there will be a massively hard crash landing at the end, the fall feels so incredibly good that it's hard to care.

"You'll be at my game tonight, right?"

I nod.

"I'll see you there."

He steps back and I exhale, able to breathe again.

I don't know how much longer I can keep this up. Even though everything in me knows giving in to my attraction to Dane will end badly, I can only spend so many nights sleeping in the same hotel room with him before I say fuck it and do it anyway.

DANE

I roll my shoulders on the elevator ride down to the lobby, my erection going down now that I'm away from Josie.

The more she resists me, the more I want her. When I got divorced, I wondered if I'd ever be able to want just one woman again. It's not smart. Keeping my options open means never being hurt and publicly humiliated again.

I never saw Josie coming, though. She started as my annoying overseer, and now? She's the focus of my every dream—all sexual. I spend more time with her than anyone and I still can't seem to get enough.

If only I could be what she needs. What she deserves. I'm a ten in the bedroom but about a three in the emotional support department. It just isn't something I've ever been good at. My ex told me that was the reason she cheated with Sam—because our relationship lacked intimacy.

She'll only be with me for another six to eight weeks, depending on how our season goes. I hate the thought of her leaving and eventually finding some other man who will get to touch her and wake up beside her every day.

It won't be one of my teammates doing it right under my nose, not after what Sam did to me.

I take a cab to the downtown deli where I'm meeting Abigail. Even though I'm five minutes early, she's already there, sitting in a booth for two with a massive smile on her face.

She squeals and stands up when I walk in, hugging me and taking a selfie of the two of us. She's wearing a jersey cut for a woman with my number on it, her red hair loose around her shoulders. "Thank you for doing this," she says, unable to stop smiling. "I've been a huge fan of yours forever."

"I appreciate it."

A server comes over to take our drink orders—unsweet tea for me and lemonade for her. I look over the menu after that, but Abigail looks at me.

"Did you already decide what you want?" I ask her.

"Oh, I'll just take anything. I don't want to waste a second I could spend looking at you."

I cringe inside. I'm just an ordinary guy who happens to be really good at hockey. It's always weird for me when people are starstruck.

"So I hear you're in medical school," I say, closing the menu. "That's great. What kind of doctor do you want to be?"

"A pediatrician."

"Wow, awesome. Med school must be super hard."

She nods. "Some of my classes have been. I like it, though."

The server returns, glancing between us expectantly. She's the opposite of starstruck with the deli so busy there's a line out the door.

"I'll have the club on wheat with potato salad," I say.

"I'll take the special," Abigail says, her gaze still on me.

The server writes down the order and disappears. I immediately wish she'd come back.

"So, have you been following the datemedane hashtag?" Abigail asks.

"Uh, no...my assistant was actually the one who saw it."

Her face lights up. "Oh. Well." She reaches across the table, her fingertips grazing my chest. "The internet is totally shipping us. And I'm free tonight for your game."

Normally, I wouldn't turn down an attractive, eager woman. Games end late and it's hard to find hookups. But Abigail doesn't do it for me because she's not Josie.

"I appreciate that, but"

She cuts me off. "I'll do anal. Or a threesome. Whatever you want, I'm down."

My lips part because...that was unexpected. I quickly put my game face back on.

"Um...I just want to have lunch."

Her expression falls. "Am I not pretty enough for you?"

I silently curse Josie for making me do this. It doesn't matter what Abigail looks like. I was never going to want more than lunch with her. But now, in her eyes, I'm the bad guy because I don't want to bring her to my hotel room tonight for group sex with me and my teammates.

"No, you're very pretty. It's just that there's someone else I'm into."

She arches her brows, looking hopeful again. "I said I'd do a threesome."

I can't help laughing as I imagine pitching that idea to Josie. "Uh, she wouldn't go for that."

Abigail recoils. "So you think I'm a slut for liking threesomes?"

I look around, feeling like I'm being punk'd or something. "I didn't say that."

She sneers. "You didn't have to. You made it clear that your precious *girlfriend*"--she air-quotes the word--"thinks she's too good for threesomes."

I put my hands up in mock surrender. "Don't put words in my mouth."

"You're an asshole!"

She throws her lemonade at me and slides out of the booth, then stomps out of the deli. People are looking at me, a couple of them recording with camera phones.

Awesome. This PR fail, for once, was not my fault.

I leave cash on the table and get up, lemonade dripping from my shirt onto the floor as I walk out. Once outside, I text Josie.

Dane: That didn't go well.

Josie: WTF?? How could it have been any easier? You make small talk over sandwiches and leave.

Dane: She wanted anal.

Josie: OMG. I am deceased...

Dane: You may see videos online of her throwing her drink on me.

Josie: Shit. I'll start damage control.

Dane: This is what you get for asking me to go out on a date with someone else...j/s

Josie: My fault for assuming you could calmly cornhole her and move on with your life I guess...

Dane: Not funny

Josie: Are you going to the arena?

Dane: Yes.

Josie: Meet you there.

Dane: Bring me a meatball sub?
Josie: Okay. Don't talk to any reporters.
Dane: Ok boss. Wear my jersey.
Josie: I might.

nineteen

JOSIE

Big hands move down my body, cupping my breasts and making me gasp. They reach my stomach, a thumb lightly dipping into my belly button before continuing down. I can't see a face, but I know it's Dane. Only he could make me feel this way.

His hands stop around my hips, gripping them as he puts his face between my thighs, his warm breath on my skin forcing the air from my chest. I press my forearms to the mattress and arch my back up, trying to get closer to his mouth.

I can't seem to talk in this dream. If I could, I'd beg him for more. I've never felt as much as I do right now. As much...what, I'm not even sure. I can't see clearly and I can't hear a thing, but what I feel is magnified many times.

The thought of him taking his hands away makes me ache. Even if this is all I get, I want him to stay. I want this closeness.

I'm awake. I breathe slowly and deeply, trying to sink back into the dream.

No luck. I'm awake now, though still aroused. The urge to go to the bathroom forces me to toss the covers aside and get out of bed.

We're in Dallas, ending the road trip that started in Chicago. The fallout from Abigail's social media posts has been minimal because several witnesses who were in the deli came forward to defend Dane and say that she was rude to him. Still, it's felt like a grind to me. I don't like the way the Mammoths' PR people roll their eyes over Dane and assume the worst.

Just because he's been a pain in the ass in the past doesn't mean he never gets the benefit of the doubt. I think the entire PR department needs a dressing down about who brings in the money that pays their salaries.

That's not my concern, though. I slowly make my way to the bathroom, running my hand along the TV stand since I can't see anything.

Dane and I have an ongoing disagreement about leaving the bathroom light on with the door cracked. I say it keeps us from tripping over things in the middle of the night when we're in a different room every time and need to use the bathroom; he says he can't sleep unless there's complete darkness. So we go back and forth.

My big toe hits a desk leg. I cringe and mutter, "Fuck you, Dane."

I've had a bruise somewhere on my body since I started this gig as his overseer. I run into chairs, desks, tables and, worst of all—the legs on bed frames. Those things hurt my toes like a mother. I lost a toenail to one.

I go into the bathroom and pee, wondering why I can't have erotic dreams about a sensible man like Lucas, who would probably have no problem with leaving the bathroom light on. After I wash my hands, I of course leave the light on and crack the door, finding my way back to bed without issue.

When I glance over at Dane's bed, the covers are pushed back and it's empty. I do a double take.

Empty.

What the actual fuck?

I walk over to the lights on the wall between the beds and switch one on, verifying that he is, in fact, not in bed.

I turn into that red guy from *Inside Out*, flames shooting from my head. I'm going to end his life with my bare hands.

When I pick up my cell phone to make sure there's not a text about an emergency with one of his teammates, my hand is shaking. He could have woken me up if there was an emergency.

There's no text.

I get dressed, not knowing where I'm going or how I'll get there. All his talk about my cute nose and how beautiful I am. If I find him with another woman, I'm going to...

My eyes well with tears and I laugh bitterly. Not that. I will not *cry* if I find him with another woman.

Get it together, Josie. Do your job.

That's the problem. I no longer know where my job ends and my personal feelings begin. I do know I'm on such thin ice with Jane that if Dane gets any bad publicity, I could easily get fired.

I can't afford that. Whether or not I deserve to be at the top of my aunt's shit list, I am.

The Mammoths players often hang out in hotel lobbies or bars when they return after going out from games. I'll go down and see if anyone has seen or heard from Dane.

I check the time on my phone on the way out the door, 2:48 a.m. That's very late for anyone to be hanging out, but it's the only idea I have. If I don't find anyone, I'll start blowing Dane's phone up with texts.

If he's not on the team plane in the morning for the flight home, it'll be both of our asses.

When the elevator doors open into the hotel lobby, a man mopping the marble floor steps aside to make way for me.

"Excuse me," I say, veering to the left to stay on the dry part of the floor.

The spacious lobby is pretty much deserted. I check the lounge areas, finding them empty.

My stomach churns with a mix of anger and frustration. We're supposed to leave for the airport at five forty-five. If I don't find him, am I supposed to get on the plane without him?

There's a "Closed" sign in front of the hotel restaurant and bar, but I walk past it to check the seats. On the last barstool, Dane's sitting with his arms folded in front of him on the bar, a bottle of water sitting off to the side.

"Hey," he says as I approach, all casual, like he didn't just spike my adrenaline.

I arch my brows. "Hey. Thanks for sending me into a panic."

"I can't sit by myself and drink some water?"

I knit my brows together. "Of course you can, but"

"Only if I ask you first?"

"Just tell me."

He scoffs, a smile tugging on the corners of his lips. "I didn't want to wake you up. And we both know if I told you I needed some air, you'd be like, What? Where? With who? I'll come with you."

I sniff and turn away, offended. "Sorry my presence is so annoying."

He laughs lightly. "You don't annoy me. I just couldn't sleep and I felt like brooding alone."

"Over what?"

He's quiet for a couple of seconds before answering. "The game. I made some stupid mistakes and we would have won if I'd been smarter."

The Mammoths lost 3–2 last night, But Dane

never mentioned anything after the game about feeling responsible for it. He just seemed quiet and down, which is always the case after a loss.

"Everyone makes mistakes," I say.

"Yeah, but this is a big fucking stage to make mistakes on."

"It still happens."

He picks up his water and sips it, looking straight ahead. "I miss my bed. I'm glad we're going home tomorrow."

"Did your teammates make you feel bad about the mistakes?"

"No, there was only one that anyone other than me noticed."

"Don't tell me you're secretly humble," I crack. "You'll shatter my image of you as a cocky, overconfident narcissist."

He laughs, smiling a genuine smile. "Nah, I'm a cocky prick for sure. I just hate letting my team down."

When he reaches for the nearly empty bowl of cocktail peanuts, I move it away before his hand gets to it.

"You might as well just cut out the middleman and go lick the inside of a toilet," I say.

He scoffs. "I already ate a bunch of them. Why stop now?"

"You don't really want these stale, germ-infested peanuts. You're emotionally eating them."

"Would you prefer I emotionally drink a bottle of whiskey?"

He leans closer to me, stretching his arm in an effort to reach the peanut bowl, but I move it farther away.

"I think you should go back to bed. We have an early flight."

His eyes darken. "Can I get in your bed?"

Warmth surges into my chest as I remember my dream. His hands on my skin. Our closeness. Everything about it was right.

"Is that really what you want?" I ask, my voice barely a whisper.

He glances at his phone, sighing heavily when he sees the time. "When do we have to leave?"

"We have to be down for breakfast at five fifteen."

His eyes narrow, the heat seeping away, replaced by aggravation.

"Then no."

I yawn and slide off my stool. "I'm going back to bed. Are you coming up or staying here?"

"I'll stay. I won't be able to sleep."

"Is there anything I can do before I go to make you feel better?"

The corners of his lips turn up in a grin. "A kiss would be nice."

I smile back. "I'd be all over it if you didn't have toilet germs in your mouth."

He groans. "I'll brush my teeth before we leave so we can snuggle on the plane."

"Are we snugglers?"

Lately, we fly with our sides pressed together, my head often on his shoulder and his hand often on my thigh. We usually have a blanket covering us, so I think of it like *what happens under the blanket, stays under the blanket.*

"Yep," he confirms.

Something inside me softens as I look at him, his hair sticking up and dark circles under his eyes from lack of sleep. Dane pretends nothing gets to him, but it's not the truth.

I step closer, inches away from him. I gently rearrange the sections of his hair that are sticking straight up, his eyes on my face as I do it.

"Did you see the Gandalf meme about me? Over the Abigail thing?" he asks.

"I missed that one."

"Apparently I'm Anal Gandalf now. *You shall not ass.*"

I burst out laughing. "Now I have to look that up as soon as I go upstairs." I cup his cheek in my hand. "Good night, Anal Gandalf."

"Night, Josie."

twenty

JOSIE

"Are you gonna make it?" I ask Dane as I drive his Range Rover from the airport to his house.

"Yeah." He closes out an app on his phone and looks over at me, the dark circles under his eyes more pronounced now. "I swear I'm more tired after that hour of sleep on the plane."

"Did you remember my cinnamon roll?"

The app he had open was a food delivery one. We decided on the flight home to order a massive amount of food for breakfast and then sleep once we got home. There are lots of errands I need to run since we've been on the road for so long, but they can wait until this afternoon.

"I got you two. Plus extra bacon since you always steal mine."

I scoff. "I had one piece one time."

"Sure you did."

"Did you remember to tell them to put your gravy on the side?"

"Yep. I'm so fucking hungry I think I'll just drink the gravy."

I turn into his long driveway, furrowing my brow when I see an unfamiliar car parked by the house.

"That's not the housekeeper's car, is it?"

He follows my gaze and groans. "Oh, fuck my life. It's my parents."

I turn to him, my eyes wide. "What? I assumed you hatched from an egg or something. You hardly ever mention your parents."

He sighs heavily, his head falling back against the passenger seat. "Guess you're about to meet Stan and Savannah."

"Are they just dropping by? Did they text?"

He glares at me. "Trust me, Nosy, if I'd known they were here, we would have gone to a hotel. My parents have the incredibly annoying habit of just flying in from Florida, unannounced, whenever they feel like it."

I fake cry as I park the car out front instead of pulling into the garage. "So much for our plan."

"We're sticking with the plan. They can entertain themselves for a while."

He gets out of the car and walks around to the back to retrieve our bags. I run a hand over my hair, wishing I didn't look like a college student who gives no fucks. I travel casual. My sweats, T-shirt, slides and messy bun scream *I woke up just in time to make it to class*.

I take the hair tie out and brush my hands through my hair, then check my teeth in my phone camera.

"You look fine. Let's go."

Dane's parents either have a key or the code, because they're already in the house, the smell of brewing coffee greeting us when we walk inside.

Dane sets our bags on the couch and we walk toward the kitchen. A beautiful woman with long dark hair walks out to greet us before we get there.

"Hello, sweetheart." She looks at me, her eyes bright. "And who is this?"

"This is my girlfriend, Josie."

His *what?* We turn to face each other, him giving

me a look of love and me giving him a look of, *What the hell?*

Savannah sighs happily, her heels clicking on the floor as she rushes over to embrace me. "Josie, he's been keeping you a secret from us! Oh Dane, she's lovely."

I try to smile, but I can't make my face look anything but panicked. "I'm a mess. We just got off a long flight."

And he just called me his girlfriend.

"You always look great, babe." Dane winks at me.

"There he is."

A tall, broad-shouldered man with salt-and-pepper hair walks into the room. I should have known that freakishly attractive Dane has freakishly attractive parents.

"He has a girlfriend, Stan." Savannah is glowing with the news.

Fake news, but still.

"Hi, I'm Josie."

Stan walks over to shake my hand, giving Dane a look of approval.

"Good for you, son."

Dane's parents both hug him and he asks, "So, what brings you guys to town?"

Stan answers. "I needed to meet a new client and we decided to come see a game and stay a couple of nights."

"You couldn't send a heads-up text or anything?"

Savannah waves a hand. "Oh, we won't be in the way. Just do whatever else you planned to do."

"Well, we ordered breakfast delivery and then we're planning to get some sleep. I've only slept an hour since Monday night."

Stan furrows his brow. "Why?"

Dane gestures at me. "Ask my insatiable girlfriend."

"Oh my god." I glare at him, my cheeks flaming.

Savannah laughs. "Oh, honey, we were young once, too. Actually, we were in Ibiza recently and Stan..." She grins, looking sheepish. "Well, let's just say he made me feel young again."

She meets her husband's gaze in a look of love and Dane groans.

"Just don't break my guest room bed again, okay?"

"That bed frame was already weak," Stan argues. "It should have easily withstood a couple of fiftysomethings having intercourse."

I force myself not to laugh because he's being serious. Dane just shakes his head.

Savannah puts her arm through mine, leading me into the kitchen. "Do you drink coffee, Josie?"

"Sometimes. I like tea better."

"I like tea, too! So tell me, how did you two meet?"

I glance back at Dane, deciding to stick with the truth. When I tell her the story about being hired to watch over him, she smiles and nods. She knows her way around Dane's kitchen, and she brews a pot of tea as we talk.

"He's always had a bit of a wild streak," she says. "But he's also fiercely loyal and he loves deeply. I'm sure you know what happened with his ex-wife."

I nod.

She lowers her voice. "It hurt him badly. Be patient with him."

Dane walks into the kitchen and pours a cup of coffee, leaning his back against the counter and giving me a look I can't read from across the room.

"Hey babe, I took our bags to the bedroom and it looks like your cat scratched the shit out of my bed frame."

Shit. None of my furniture is valuable, but

Dane's is a different story. Poor Mr. Darcy has been left alone here for long stretches while we travel, with just the housekeeper checking in on him.

I feel a little bit bad. But also not that bad because he put me in a weird spot when he told his parents I was his girlfriend. How is that going to play out over the next few days?

I smile at Savannah. "Dane absolutely loves my cat, Mr. Darcy. They snuggle constantly and rub noses. It's so cute."

Savanah's jaw drops. "That's...amazing. Dane, you've always hated cats."

His gaze is locked onto mine, amusement dancing in his eyes. "Well, if my girl loves Mr. Darcy, so do I."

Our food delivery arrives and Stan announces that he and Savannah are heading out for a few hours of shopping. As soon as they're out the door, I give Dane my best death glare.

"Your girlfriend? Really?"

He grins. "Come on, Nosy. You liked it."

I scoff. "I was not prepared to meet your parents like this. Look at me."

"You look cute. And that's how they are. They just drop in."

I bite into a piece of bacon, feeling stabby. "I'll

pretend to be your girlfriend, but you'd better kiss my cat's ass. I meant it about rubbing noses. Get on your phone and order some gourmet treats. Make him feel like the only cat in the world, Foster."

"Fine." His tone is sulky. "But I get unlimited ass grabbing."

I laugh. "You want to grab my ass in front of your parents? Classy."

"I didn't say in front of them. Whenever I want. In fact, I get unlimited everything short of actual sex."

My body heats in response to his words. I swallow hard, not just because it's Dane and I'm undeniably attracted to him, but because it's been a long time since any man has so much as accidentally brushed against my tit.

"Are you saying I have to give you unlimited blow jobs?"

"No...unless you want to?" He arches his brows and grins wickedly. "Everything else, though. No fucking, no blow jobs, but anything else."

I consider. "What about anal? Fisting? Bondage?"

He scoffs. "Jesus Christ, Nosy. Am I wearing a leather mask with just a mouth hole here? No, none of that. You know what I'm talking about."

I nod, my skin tingling at the prospect of having his hands on me. "Okay."

"Is there something I need to know about you? Are you into that stuff?"

I laugh. "I don't think so. I mean, absolutely not on fisting. And I don't want to be chained to a dingy cellar wall or anything, but a man who's...I don't know...*insistent* about what he wants is pretty hot."

The dark hunger swirling in his eyes makes my heart pound erratically. I was tired before, but now? All I can think of is his wide shoulders and his carved muscles. All the times I've watched him sleeping shirtless in hotel rooms and fantasized about being curled up to his powerful chest.

"Insistent might be putting it mildly with me," he murmurs.

I take a bite of my cinnamon roll, deliberately moaning softly when the sweet flavor hits my tongue. "Mmm, so good."

"First time I've ever been hard while eating biscuits and gravy. Thanks for that."

I pick up my plate. "I'm going to clean up and take a shower."

"Leave it. I'll clean up."

Our gazes lock. My pulse pounds and I know this is it. Something is about to change between us.

It's still a bad idea because of my job. I'm still probably setting myself up for heartbreak. But it's the way Dane makes me feel about *me* that makes me unable to deny our attraction any longer.

He makes me feel sexy. Smart. Clever. Worthy. We may not last forever, but I want to wrap my arms around those feelings and hold them close for as long as I can.

twenty-one

JOSIE

WHEN I STEP OUT OF THE BATHROOM, DANE'S waiting for me, his gaze locking with mine.

I tighten my hold on the towel I wrapped around myself after my shower; it's the only thing keeping him from seeing all of me. After all these weeks of being together twenty-four seven, he's seen more of me than any man ever has in every nonphysical way.

He's heard me snore. Seen me cranky. Watched me vomit countless times. And still, he's looking at me like I'm the most beautiful woman in the world right now. I don't want to shatter that image by losing my hold on this towel and having him find out my stomach's not rock hard like his.

"Are we..." My voice barely registers.

He moves closer and I instinctively back up, my back hitting the hallway wall. But he doesn't stop. Desire swims in his eyes as he cups my cheek and leans his forehead against mine, gently tugging on the end of a wet strand of my hair.

"I've wanted this since the first time I saw you," he rumbles, his lips so close to mine I can feel the warmth of his breath.

"The first time?"

"Hell yes. I only hated the idea of you, Josie. But the way you stood up to me..." He puts his palm on my thigh and I inhale sharply. "You refuse to take my shit. No one's ever done that." He slides his hand up around the back of my thigh, hiking it up around his waist. "I don't just want you. I *need* you."

He showered before we left the hotel this morning. I can smell a hint of his pine-tree-scented soap. I want more. More of his scent, his words, his skin. I grip a handful of his T-shirt and tug, urging him on.

His lips settle against mine at the same time his massive palm grips my ass, my squeal becoming a moan. My mouth yields to his, his tongue sweeping against mine. I let go of my towel to wrap my hand around his neck, gasping as I feel the towel getting looser.

"Don't," he says as I reach for it.

"Dane..." My heart hammers nervously.

"Let me see you. I've waited so fucking long."

He threads his fingers into mine and gently pins one of my hands to the wall, then does the same to the other. My chest rises and falls as I breathe hard, terrified of him seeing me naked in broad daylight.

"I'm average," I say weakly. "I'm not like you."

He hums a note of amusement. "You are anything but average."

I lean my head back, rolling my eyes up toward the ceiling as I exhale heavily. He opens my towel all the way, my back the only thing holding it against the wall.

I'm so not prepared for this. I shaved my legs and pits in the shower, but my lady bits haven't been waxed in ages.

"Fucking finally," he says in a low tone, cupping one of my breasts. "I've wanted to get my mouth on these forever."

He bends, lowering his tongue to one of my nipples, and I arch my back, my inhibitions forgotten. The towel drops to the floor, but who fucking cares? He's licking, sucking and tugging my nipples between his teeth in a way that I can somehow feel between my thighs.

Ragged exhales are all I can manage as he teases them, moving my hands above my head and holding my wrists with just one of his hands. He's so big, his body towering over mine in a way that feels deliciously overwhelming.

His free hand cups my breast, working in tandem with his mouth. He knows how to apply exactly the right amount of pressure to my nipples to send sparks of arousal shooting through me without causing pain. I had no idea having them pinched and nibbled on felt this good.

I'm starting to wonder if it's possible to orgasm from nipple stimulation when his hand slides down from holding my wrists. He kisses his way down my stomach and I gasp, wishing we were in the dark.

He's on his knees, looking up at me with a reverent expression. His hands cradle my hips and a devilish smirk plays on his face as he says, "Spread your feet apart, gorgeous."

Holy. Shit. Right here in the hallway? I bite my lip, holding back a nervous laugh.

His full smirk appears. "You'll spread 'em soon enough."

He buries his face between my thighs, tonguing my clit. I gasp, my palms hitting the wall. I want to feel self-conscious, but the way he's swirling his tongue...I'm lost in the sensation. My hips are in his hands and he's devouring me, his mouth every bit as skilled here as it was on my breasts.

He was right. I quickly find myself moving my feet apart to allow him more access, shamelessly grinding my hips, moving against his face as I feel the first orgasm I've had in a very long time about to rock through me.

"Oh god, Dane," I pant. "Don't stop. Please don't stop."

He doesn't, and I practically ride his face as I come apart, crying out with satisfaction.

When my body goes limp, he finally stands up, wiping my arousal from his face with his T-shirt.

"Why are you still dressed?" I ask him.

"I won't be for long."

He grins and pulls his T-shirt off over his head, then kicks off his shoes and pushes his shorts and boxers off. I look from his impressive, rock-hard erection to his face and then back to his erection again.

"You okay?" he asks, arching a brow.

"Try not to poke a hole in my uterus with that."

He laughs, putting an arm around my shoulder and another behind my knees to pick me up and carry me. "No holes, I promise."

He walks us into his bedroom, where Mr. Darcy is lying in the center of the bed. Dane ignores him and kisses me softly before setting me down, my cat jumping off the bed.

When he reaches into a bedside drawer for a condom and puts it on, I finally get to stare openly at his body. I've gotten glimpses in the locker room, but I had to pretend I wasn't interested.

He's all muscle, dark hair lightly covering his chest and trailing down. I feel a sudden stab of jealousy toward any woman who's ever touched his body. I'm greedy, wanting to explore every inch of him and never, ever share.

When he puts a knee on the bed, he pauses, looking at me. A wave of self-consciousness hits and I jump off the bed and get under the covers.

He shakes his head and grabs the top of the covers, prying them from my hands and pulling them all the way down to the end of the bed so he can see me. I close my legs and he climbs onto the bed on his knees, easing them apart. He's between my legs, looking at me with a wolfish grin.

"Why are you being shy? Can't you see how much I want you?"

His erection juts out like a sword, long and strong.

"No one's ever looked at me like this," I admit. "It's always been more of an in-the-dark, over really quick kind of thing."

He picks up one of my ankles and kisses it, caressing my calf. "Not anymore. You're too beautiful not to look at. You told me not to stop earlier. I'll never stop. You'll always come first."

There's a flutter in my stomach as he sets my foot back on the bed and leans forward, kissing my lips. "I haven't wanted any other woman since I saw you, Josie. I need to know you want me, too."

My heart swells for this beautiful, damaged man. He's been hurt, but he's still willing to expose himself to me and risk being hurt again.

"I do," I say against his lips. "I..."

"What?"

"Never mind."

He leans up on his elbows, looking down at me. "Tell me what you were going to say."

I flush, embarrassed. "I was looking at you

earlier and thinking...I hate any other woman who's ever touched you. I know it's irrational."

He smiles, his eyes crinkling at the corners. "I get it. I feel the same way about any man who's ever touched you."

"Yeah?"

He kisses me. "Yeah."

I wrap my legs around his waist, pulling him down. "What's a girl gotta do around here to get fucked?"

His amused smile slides away as he pushes himself inside me, not stopping to make sure I'm comfortable.

"Ah, that's...big." I shift.

"You wanted to fuck and I aim to please." He pulls out and goes all the way back in at full force.

"Fuck. Slow down. I haven't had sex in a long time and you're used to groupies with gaping vaginas."

He pulls all the way out, scowling. "You want me to fill that smart mouth up? Because I can do that."

I bite my lip, smiling. "All I'm saying is slow down. Let me adjust. Appreciate the tightness of my inexperience."

Amusement dances in his eyes, but he doesn't say a word.

He kisses me gently and pushes himself in, more slowly this time. I thread my fingers into his hair and he buries his face in my neck, kissing me until he finds my most sensitive spot, right beneath my earlobe. Soon, he's buried completely inside me, my legs locked around his waist.

"You feel so fucking good, baby," he says in my ear.

He gets on his knees, putting my ankles on his shoulders, and I immediately miss the closeness of him. But from here, he's able to play with my clit as he thrusts into me, and *damn*, is he good at it.

I feel myself climbing toward climax again, but what I want more than anything is to see him lose control.

"Show me what you like," I say. "Please. Fuck me the way you like it."

"I will, baby. After you come."

He keeps thrusting, his fingers circling. When I see his strained expression, holding back his own arousal in favor of mine, I let go, coming even harder than I did the first time. It seems to go on and on, Dane's expert fingers making it last.

"Keep your legs here," he says, and I lock my ankles behind his head.

He leans over me again, one hand bracing himself on his headboard, and he pistons his hips, pumping into me so hard I have to put a hand against the headboard to keep myself in place.

His arm muscles flex as he thrusts, breathing hard. He's spectacular. I've never seen anything so masculine and sexy in my life. I can't believe I'm the one having this effect on him. I know I'll be sore from this tomorrow and I'm going to love every second of it.

"Oh, fuck..." His eyes lock onto mine as he rocks his hips into me, moving faster now. "Josie."

God, I love the sound of my name on his lips as his body locks and he groans with his release. His body shudders and I run my palms down his sweat-slicked back.

He exhales, relaxing, and we lie down side by side.

"We've been dancing around this thing between us for a long time," he says softly.

"Was it worth the wait?" I stroke my fingertips over his cheek.

"I think so. But let's dispense with this pretend girlfriend thing."

The flutter returns to my stomach. "I'm not sure what you mean."

"No more games. I want you in my life as my girlfriend."

I love the sound of that. And I hate that I have to worry about what my aunt would say, but I do.

"I don't know how that would work with my job."

His hand is on my hip, his thumb stroking my skin. "We can keep it private until you're done with the job. But then we tell everyone."

I smile, feeling like a flower about to burst into bloom. "Okay."

There are so many unknowns, but I'm sure of the most important thing: us.

twenty-two

DANE

I WAS DREAMING ABOUT BACON. PROBABLY BECAUSE Josie and I finally—fucking *finally*—had sex, and now I can dream about other things. I shift in bed, open my eyes and sniff the air.

It wasn't a dream. I smell bacon, and Josie's curled up asleep beside me, so she's not the one making it.

My mom. It comes back to me then—my parents are here and she must be cooking. I grab my phone from the bedside table to see how long Josie and I slept. It's 6:07 p.m. We've been out for almost seven hours.

I'm groggy and could easily go back to sleep.

"No!" Josie cries, flying into a sitting position, her eyes wide.

"Easy," I say, amused.

She exhales hard and puts a palm on her chest. "I was having a dream that I had to chase you out a bathroom window."

I cringe, feigning heart pain. "Damn, my technique needs some work if that's what you're dreaming about after this morning."

She smiles. "This morning was amazing and you know it, Foster."

Stretching out on her side next to me, she leans on her elbow. I've seen her fresh out of bed, her face clean and her hair rumpled, but never this close up. It's the first time I've noticed a tiny freckle just above her right eyebrow.

"You won't have to chase me anywhere anymore." My cock is hard and ready for more of her. "I'll be the one chasing you out windows."

She tries to cover the flicker of doubt that passes over her face, but I don't miss it. I get why she's skeptical, given my reputation. But the closer I get to Josie, the more I want. She's not some woman I met after a game, screwed, and don't plan to get a number from.

"Something smells really good," she says, lowering her brows.

I run my hand up the back of her bare thigh, groaning with satisfaction when I find her ass bare. She put on one of my T-shirts before we went to sleep, and apparently, nothing else.

"Mom's cooking something." I lean over and kiss her neck. "We can go eat in a little bit."

Her soft laughter is warm on my ear. "Or we can go now."

I slide my hand beneath the shirt, my palm coasting up her stomach to cup her breast. She inhales softly.

"Tell me you don't like this," I say as I gently pinch her nipple between my thumb and forefinger.

"Dane..." she protests weakly as her nipple stiffens.

"Mm-hmm..." I kiss the spot beneath her ear that made her crazy earlier. "Do it, baby. Tell me we can't because my parents are in the other room."

"They are," she whispers.

I pull the shirt up, expose her breasts, and suck one of her nipples into my mouth for a few seconds, then nip at it, eliciting a little gasp.

"I know," I whisper back. "But I'm not letting

my girl out of here with a wet, needy pussy." I move her hand to my rock-hard erection. "And you're the only one who can do something about this."

"Dane..."

I flick my tongue over her nipple, still a perfectly stiff pink peak. She wraps her hand around my cock and it's all I can do not to groan hard at how good it feels.

"I can't come with your parents in the other room," she says softly in my ear.

The fuck she can't. I don't back down from any challenge. With a smirk, I kiss her and say, "Better grab a pillow to scream into."

I move down and get to work, not wasting a single second.

Her body is soft and warm, her pussy like honey on my tongue. It's actually not work at all to tongue fuck her and lick and suck her folds—I could do this for hours. I love the way she squirms, trying to stay silent as I bring her to the edge of climax and then keep my mouth away from her clit, instead inserting two fingers inside her.

She's breathing hard, one of her hands twining into my hair and tugging. If we were alone, I'd play this game with her for a while, making her come hard after at least thirty minutes of edging. But since time is a factor, I return my mouth to her clit, sucking it while I fuck her with my fingers.

It only takes a few seconds for her to buck her hips against me and come, her body tensing and no sound coming from her open mouth.

When she finally relaxes and exhales hard, I grin at her. "Damn, you were quiet."

"It wasn't easy," she whispers.

"Can I bend you over the bathroom counter?" I ask, desperate to watch myself fuck her.

"We'll smell like rubber," she says softly.

"No, we won't."

"I could always smell rubber when my college roommate got home from her boyfriend's place." She bites her lip nervously. "Have you been tested for STIs since the last time you slept with someone?"

I consider. "Yeah, the team doctor tests us every six weeks. I'm good."

"I'm on the pill."

Oh, fuck. My cock twitches at the thought of being buried deep inside her without a condom. I haven't done that since I was married because I haven't had anything but one-night stands.

"Are you sure?"

She nods. "It's totally fine if you don't want to.

I've been test"

"I fucking want to."

Desire for her surges through my body, but I stop myself and kiss her, soft and slow. Josie is putting a lot of trust in me, and that means more than the sex.

When the kiss ends, I lean my forehead against hers and she whispers, "Tell me you want me, Dane."

Those words just don't cover it. If I said *I want you*, it would be too much of an understatement. I don't know if there are words that will convey how I feel, but she wants me to say something, and I will.

"When you're close to me, I need to touch you," I say against her lips. "I need it so fucking much. Like I need air. Now that I've made you come, I need that, too. I need this closeness. I need to be the only man you touch and kiss. I need to be...enough for you. Everything. I need you to crave me even half as much as I crave you."

She runs her fingertips over my skin, up my bicep to my shoulder, then to my cheek, which she cups in her hand.

"I need it, too," she whispers. "I'm scared of needing it...but I do."

She slides from the bed and reaches for my

hand. I follow her into the bathroom, closing the door behind us and turning on the shower to mask the sound. She looks up into my eyes and pulls the T-shirt over her head and off, dropping it to the floor.

I can feel her shrinking beneath my gaze, which is the last thing I want. I thread my fingers through hers on both hands.

"You are so damn sexy, Josie Garver. I fantasize about your body constantly."

I take a step forward, backing her into the counter. She watches with wide eyes as I slide my hand down her thigh, past her knee, all the way to her ankle. I lift it, trying to put it on the counter, but she's too short for that, so I have to set her ass on the counter and then put her foot on it off to the side.

"Dane, what are you—oh *god*." She closes her eyes as I slide two fingers back into her.

"Do you have any idea how fucking hot I am for this pussy? I caught a glance of this dark pussy hair when you were coming out of the shower one day and I've jerked off thinking about it so many times. I want to fuck this pussy, eat this pussy, finger this pussy and play with this pussy until you can't take anymore."

Her mouth opens in a silent *O* as I use my thumb to circle her clit.

"It's too sensitive," she says in a pleading tone.

"No one but me touches this pussy. Say it."

"Dane, please…"

"Say it."

She whimpers, squirming. "No one but you touches my pussy."

"That's right, baby." I pull my fingers out and get her down from the counter.

Palming my cock, I say, "And this is yours. For as long as you want me, no other woman even gets a second look."

She nods and licks her lips, then turns around and puts her palms on the counter. Our eyes meet in the mirror and she says, "So then give me what's mine."

I've wanted her to look at me this way for so long, and I wasn't sure she ever would. My whole body is tense with built-up longing for her, our earlier sex only satisfying a small fraction of it.

I line my cock up at her entrance and watch her face in the mirror as I slide in, her lips parting. It's heaven, getting to watch her expression as I slide in and out of her. To see her tits bouncing.

She's so tight and wet that I have to go slowly,

savoring each thrust into her. Steam is clouding the mirror, but I can still see her face, and the deeper I go, the more she likes it.

I ease her shoulder back until her back is flush against my chest. She moans softly when I tease one of her nipples as I fuck her, sliding my other hand down so my fingers can circle her clit.

She doesn't have to say a word. I can feel her orgasm coming, her pussy clenching around my cock. It's fucking amazing to be buried inside her as she comes, trying to stay silent and failing.

She turns her head back and I kiss her, her mouth hungry and sated at the same time.

"Come for me," she says softly.

Fuck yes.

She bends over and puts her palms on the counter. I put one hand on her hip and another on her shoulder, her pussy so soaked now that my cock makes sounds as I thrust in and out of her.

I fuck her deeper and harder, wishing it could last forever. Her pussy is too sweet for that, though. In just a couple of minutes, she's milking my cock dry as I hold myself inside her, not letting out the shuddering groan I would if my parents weren't here.

I get a washcloth from the closet inside the

bathroom and wet it with warm water, cleaning her up. She smiles and kisses me.

"We should get out there."

I grin. "You so obviously just got railed. I love it."

"Really?"

"Honestly, nothing could make my parents happier. Don't worry about it."

She smooths a hand over her hair. "It feels a little weird."

"Trust me, babe. Stan and Savannah just want their son to be happy. I think my mom's making her killer bacon and cheddar dip. Are you hungry?"

"I'm starving."

"Let's go find some clothes and catch up with my folks."

I find her a Mammoths T-shirt and a pair of sweats with a tie at the waist, grabbing a T-shirt and sweats for myself. When she walks out of the bathroom, dressed and holding her phone, her expression is crestfallen.

"What's wrong?" I ask.

She looks up at me, on the verge of tears. "Monica got the promotion."

twenty-three

JOSIE

"Honey, this aunt of yours sounds very toxic," Savannah says, picking up my plate from the table. "Let me get you some more lasagna."

I shoot Dane a look, already stuffed like a Thanksgiving turkey from loading up on his mom's crackers and dip appetizer and her cheesy, carby, comforting lasagna.

"Mom, she's full," he says. "But I'll take more."

Savannah looks at me, a line between her brows. "You'll take a little bit more, won't you?"

"Sure," I concede, grateful I'm wearing pants with a stretchy waistband.

She gives me an approving smile and heads back over to the counter.

Stan moves his napkin from his lap to the table, clearing his throat. "She sounds quite unprofessional to me. That news should have been delivered to you by her in a face-to-face conversation."

"You know, this could be reverse nepotism," Savannah says as she loads Dane's plate up with lasagna. "I saw a psychiatrist being interviewed about it a few weeks ago. It was fascinating. It's where family members treat family who work for them extra harshly to avoid the appearance of special treatment."

I've always thought of my relationship with my aunt as complicated, but I'm not so sure it is. Jane is my father's sister and she always hated my mom because my mom left my dad when I was little because his drinking had become a problem. We moved far away from him and his family and he drank himself to death a few years after. My mom told me we could go to his funeral if I wanted to, but she was honest with me that his family blamed her for his death and it could be uncomfortable. I chose not to go.

Dane puts a hand on my knee beneath the

table, meeting his mom's gaze as she sets my plate back down in front of me.

"What's new with you, Mom?" he asks. "Did you find anything when you went shopping today?"

I give him a grateful glance as Savannah excitedly tells him about a vase she bought from a downtown art gallery. Even though I don't want to talk about not getting the promotion, being in his parents' company feels as comforting as the food Dane's mom made for us. They're parental like my mom was, but also *not* so parental in ways that make me laugh inwardly.

"Sweetie, why was that young woman on Twitter saying you anal shamed her?" Savannah asks as we're all cleaning up after dinner.

My eyes widen, but I don't let my reaction show. My mother never would have said the word *anal* to me.

"I think it's called X now, dear," Stan says.

"Because she offered me anal sex and I said no, Mom."

"Well, I hope you said *no, thank you*. And you didn't really shame her about it, did you?"

A corner of Dane's mouth curves up as he meets my gaze. He's loading clean silverware into a drawer while I wipe off the table.

"You have to be firm with puck bunnies," he says. "I accidentally left my car unlocked in the player lot one time and there was a naked woman in my back seat after a game. She sent her clothes with a friend, so I'd look like an asshole if I just kicked her out into the cold."

I gape at him, imagining that scene playing out. Being naked in a stranger's car sounds hellish to me.

"What did you do?" Stan asks.

"I called security. They brought out a blanket and dragged her out of my car."

Savannah starts loading dishes into the dishwasher, shaking her head in disbelief. "Let's talk about something more pleasant. How did the two of you meet?"

Dane closes the drawer and turns to face me, grinning as he crosses his arms. "Josie was hired as my personal bodyguard."

Stan frowns. "Your what now?"

I smile at him. "I'm a publicist. Dane's team owner thought he could use some...individual oversight."

That makes Stan laugh heartily. "I like her, Dane."

"She's pretty damn likable."

Dane's eyes are warm as he looks at me, making Monica and the promotion feel like less of a thing. Not making it to senior publicist means I'm still broke, but other than that, it doesn't mean as much to me as I thought it would. Now that I have more in my life than just my job—so much more because of Dane—I know I'll be okay, senior publicist or not.

"I think Josie should start her own business," Dane says. "She's got a great mind for it."

"I think that's an excellent idea," Stan says. "Especially now."

I shake my head. "Dane's overestimating me. I wouldn't know where to begin."

"You've already got a top-tier client on your roster." He winks at me.

I raise my index finger and point it at him. "Actually, I don't. My aunt's firm does, and I'm the employee she assigned."

Dane considers. "A technicality. I'm sure Arnold will hire Josie Garver PR if you keep giving him the same results."

I laugh. "So I'll have one client that I work for around the clock? Who is also..." I can't bring myself to say the words *my boyfriend*. "...more than just a client."

"I might be able to behave myself without you for a few hours a day while you do other work."

Savannah scoffs, amused. "Pardon my French, but grow the fuck up, son. If you want to be in an adult relationship, you have to act like an adult."

He grins at her. "I know, Mom. I'm just teasing her. She knows I've got her back." He turns to me, his expression shifting to a serious one. "I'll provide the startup cash and help you drum up a few clients. Arnold will give you a glowing recommendation. You need to do this."

All three of them are looking at me expectantly. I still haven't had time to think about Monica getting the promotion and what that means for me. A little voice inside my head is telling me to wait until my assignment with Dane is finished and then reassess things. Because while I appreciate Dane believing in me, I know if I started my own publicity business, my aunt would use every resource at her disposal to see that I fail at it.

Why have I been so loyal to someone who would do that to me? Whether she's the only family I have left or not, she doesn't deserve it.

Savannah stifles a yawn. Dane walks over to the refrigerator and takes out two bottles of water, side-eyeing me as Mr. Darcy jumps up onto the kitchen counter.

"We're going to head to bed," he says. "You guys know where everything is. I have to be at the arena early for game day. You're coming to the game, right?"

"Of course, we wouldn't miss it," Savannah says. "I might spend some time here tomorrow while your father is working."

Dane hugs her and kisses her on the cheek. I like how openly affectionate he is with her.

Everyone says good night and a wave of exhaustion hits me as we walk to Dane's bedroom, his hand on the small of my back. It's been a hell of a day. Dane and I *slept together*. Several times. Our pretend relationship didn't last long, and now we seem to be in a real one.

What does that mean, though? Are we exclusive?

I also met his parents, who weren't at all what I expected, though I didn't really have any expectations because I never thought I'd meet his parents.

And Monica got the promotion. I want to be angry about it, but more than anything, I'm hurt. I'm good at my job. I've put in my time and contributed a lot of good ideas. My clients all love my work.

After we've brushed our teeth and climbed into bed, I'm grateful when Dane wraps his arms around me instead of trying to initiate sex again. The sex was amazing, but I'm sexed out.

It's sinking in that this time with him won't last forever, and soon I'll have to walk back into the office and congratulate Monica on her new role. I may choke on those words.

"Josie Garver PR has a nice ring to it," Dane says, kissing the top of my head.

I close my eyes and burrow against his chest, tucking my head beneath his chin. "I can't even think about that right now. Hold me tighter."

He strengthens his hold on me, making me feel secure.

"Better?" he murmurs.

"Mm-hmm."

Jane is going to have to reassign me somehow because there's no way I can work on a team led by Monica. I'll quit before I report to that bitch. I'd rather eat cat food and sleep in a tent than give her the satisfaction. I can always fall back on waitressing. And I may have to do it soon.

"You think you guys will make the playoffs?"

"Yep."

I sigh, relaxing a little. That gives me more time with Dane. More time for the shock of losing the promotion to wear off. More time before I have to go back to the office and face reality.

twenty-four

DANE

"On your left, Foster!"

I turn just in time to raise my knee and deflect a soccer ball someone kicked my way. My teammates are gathered in a circle outside the locker room, passing the ball around to loosen up before our game.

"Where are you going?" Tate asks as I kick it back his way and turn to leave.

"Meeting," I call over my shoulder.

As of now, I'm the only one who knows about the meeting, but it's happening. Our team owner,

Arnold, is in the arena for the game, and I'd rather talk to him in person than over the phone.

"There he is! Our hottest scorer!" One of the security guards, Mel, holds his fist out and I give him a bump.

"Hey, what's new, Mel?"

"My daughter's sleeping four hours in a row now, so life is good, bro. My wife loves that swing and stroller you guys sent over, along with a year's worth of diapers! You guys are way too good to me."

I grin and point at him. "She better be wearing that Mammoths outfit we put in there. She's got it on right now, right?"

He laughs heartily. "Bro, of course she's got it on right now. I told Marcie that goes straight into the washer when it gets peed or puked on. We don't mess around with game day. She's got her purple and black on."

"Nice."

Other than kicking in some money, I had nothing to do with the gifts—Aiden's wife, Jenn, takes care of that stuff. But it's a team tradition that every baby gift includes Mammoths team clothing.

"You guys gonna get that *W* tonight?"

"Planning on it."

"Get dirty if you got to." Mel shadowboxes as I round the corner and lose sight of him.

With less than three hours until game time, I only have a few minutes to talk to Arnold. The pregame meal our team chef makes before games will be served soon, and I always eat it on time. Then I have to stretch and get dressed.

One of Arnold's assistants, Carol, is looking at something on her phone when I walk into the suite where her desk sits outside the door to his office.

"Dane Foster, what's this I hear about a cute PR girl whipping you into shape?" She smiles knowingly.

"What can I say? I'm a sucker for a good whipping," I quip. "Can I get five minutes with the boss man?"

She frowns. "Ooh, that'll be tough. He's got friends in town for the game. Can I pass a message on for you?"

I can't get Josie's hurt expression out of my head. Her aunt blindsided her, treated her like shit and made her question her worth. That's not gonna fly on my watch.

"It's important," I tell Carol. "Come on, Mama C. We all know you're the one who's really in charge around here. Get me five minutes with the boss and I'll owe you one."

The corners of her lips turn up in a smile. "Well...I can try. But no promises."

She gets up and walks over to Arnold's solid wood door, knocking twice.

"Come in," Arnold calls.

He and two other men are laughing about something when Carol opens the door.

"Dane Foster would like five minutes," she says, taking a step inside the office. "I thought I'd take your guests to get the jerseys and hats you mentioned."

"Sure," Arnold says. "Tell Dane to come on in."

He introduces me to his friends and I recognize both of their names as big donors to the Mammoths' team foundation. Of course I say yes when they ask for photos with me, getting Arnold in the best possible mood before I ask him for a favor.

Once we're alone and the door is closed, his smile is more subdued. We haven't spoken since he hired Josie to watch over me, and our conversation about that wasn't exactly friendly. I'm not good at swallowing my pride, but for Josie, I do it anyway.

"You were right about me," I say as I sit down

in a chair across from the leather sofa he's seated on. "My focus wasn't where it needed to be."

That's as close as he's getting to an apology from me, but it seems good enough. He nods, his expression relaxing.

"Josie seems to be a good fit. You're in the zone. And for you to come to me like this..." He scoffs. "This is a side of you I've never seen, and I appreciate it, Dane. I hope there are no hard feelings."

I nod. "Josie is actually why I came to see you."

"You want me to let her go?"

"No," I say more forcefully than I intended.

He gives me a knowing smile. "I heard the two of you have a very friendly relationship."

I pause before saying, "That's true."

"I plan to keep her on through the end of the season, but if you're here to ask me to make her a permanent hire, I can't do that. I'd have all the players asking me to put their girlfriends on the payroll."

There's always a note of condescension in his tone, and it's all I can do not to bite back and tell him I'm not a fucking idiot who expects him to pay my girlfriend to travel with the team full time. But that won't get me what I want. I take a deep breath, keeping my expression neutral.

"Of course. You've been more than generous helping me get back on track already."

Fuck. My ego is taking a major beating today. I don't suck up to anyone, but that's exactly what I'm doing right now.

This is for Josie. I imagine myself giving her the good news, and it helps me keep shoveling down this humble pie.

"Josie was in line for a promotion and it went to someone else," I say, hoping my direct approach will work. "She deserved to get it. I'm asking you, as a favor to me, to end the contract with JG Publicity and give it to Josie instead. It won't change anything, really. She'll finish out the season, but then she'll have something great to put on her résumé for all her hard work."

Arnold arches his brows. "Her hard work getting you in line by sleeping with you?"

I tense, my right hand instinctively closing into a fist. It's all I can do not to lunge at him and grab him by his perfectly pressed dress shirt so I can wipe that smug look off his face.

"That's what you think of her?" I don't even try to hide the menace from my tone.

He puts his hands up, the tone in the room tight and tense now.

"Look, whatever she's doing to keep you out of trouble, I'm glad it's working. But I've been a client of Jane Garver's PR firm for many years, and I'm not dropping her just because her niece was passed over for a promotion."

Why did I think he'd help Josie? Arnold's a self-centered prick. I fucking hate that I lowered myself before him and he dismissed me like a fly buzzing around his steak.

"I guess we're done here, then," I say, standing up.

"Let's get a win tonight."

Like he's the one out there getting rammed into the boards and punched. I want to tell him to suck my dick, but this isn't the right time. He'd probably fire Josie immediately just to spite me, and I won't risk that.

I'm not shaking his hand. I'll lie my ass off and thank him for seeing me, but I'm not shaking that asshole's hand.

"Keep up the good work, Dane. No more park benches."

He flashes me a too-white smile and points at me. I force myself to smile back, hoping the universe has at least given him erectile dysfunction.

"We're back," Carol says, coming into the room with Arnold's friends.

"I have to go," I say quickly. "Pregame stuff to do."

I wave at everyone and make a hasty exit.

So much for my plan to save the day for Josie, I hate this feeling of helplessness.

Somehow, though, I have to find a way to focus on the game. Not for Arnold, but for my teammates. And also because the longer we make it into the postseason, the longer I get to be with Josie twenty-four seven.

twenty-five

JOSIE

I SMILE AT DANE AS HE WALKS INTO THE BEDROOM, a towel wrapped around his waist, his hair wet from a shower.

"I guess I should shower again, too. So I don't go to the arena smelling like sex."

He grins playfully. "I like you smelling like sex. Put on one of my sweaters, too. Every male creature will know you're spoken for, even the blind ones, because they'll smell me on you."

"Gross." I laugh at his reasoning. "I'm not considering mating with a dog or anything, caveman."

"You feeling better?"

I woke up with his head between my thighs. How could I feel anything but amazing? After a round of oral that nearly made me pull his hair out, he made me come a second time with long, slow sex. Dane is making me into a morning person.

"I'm good. You're right. It's just a job. I still get to be with you. Once the season is over, I can look for another job."

I get out of bed, Dane catching me around the waist to stop me for a kiss. Something inside me tightens at the way he's looking at me. This is really happening. My aunt can ruin my career, but she can't ruin *this*.

He kisses me harder, dropping the towel. I feel his erection against my stomach, thick and insistent. Reluctantly, I pull away.

"I have to shower before we go. So we can keep going here, but I'm showering after and that means we'll be late."

He makes a growly sound of disapproval against my lips. "We have ten minutes. Eight to fuck, two to shower."

"I can't shower and get dressed in two minutes."

Another growly sound. I kiss him and turn to walk to the bathroom. He smacks my ass as I go, the sting making arousal swirl low in my stomach even as I glare at him.

"Not my fault," he says, putting his hands up in mock surrender. "Your ass is too tempting and that's on you."

I roll my eyes, quickly grab clean clothes and walk into the bathroom. His constant interest in my body secretly thrills me. No matter what I'm wearing or what I'm doing, he thinks I'm sexy. He doesn't care if my body is perfect; he loves it exactly as it is.

As I wash myself in the shower, I can't help wishing it was his hands on me instead. I avoid getting my hair wet since I don't have enough time to dry it.

When I emerge from the bathroom dressed in black leggings, a dark-purple tunic and black boots, Dane looks like an ad for the dark suit he's wearing. It's cut to define his body just right, a pressed white dress shirt beneath the jacket and a plain red tie.

"You want a sandwich?" he asks as he passes me a travel mug of coffee.

I look at my watch. "No, we have to go."

The doorbell rings and we give each other a look of confusion. His parents left yesterday and we aren't expecting any deliveries.

"I should answer it," he says, his brows lowered. "It could be a photographer. You stay out of view."

"If it's a photographer, they're trespassing."

"Trust me, I'll let them know."

We both walk toward the front door and I stand off to the side, out of view. He opens the door, his expression perturbed.

"Can I help you?"

"Hi Dane, I'm Monica Allen, your new representative from JG Publicity."

My heart stutters in my chest. This can't be happening.

"I don't understand," Dane says, glaring at her. "I didn't request anyone new and I want to keep working with Josie."

"Josie's been reassigned." Monica steps into the house uninvited. "Your home is beautiful."

Dane and I exchange a concerned look. This is an unexpected development, to say the least. Even more unexpected than not getting the promotion.

Monica is admiring the house when her gaze lands on me. "Josie? What are you doing hiding there like a stalker?"

"I wasn't hiding."

"You need to leave, Monica," Dane says.

She turns her plastic smile on him. "JG

Publicity has a contract with the Mammoths and I've been assigned to be your personal publicist for the remainder of the season." Then she turns the smile on me. "Josie, Jane wants you to report back to the office immediately."

With my tail between my legs, I'm sure. Monica is loving this. I want to smack the smug smile off her face.

"No." Dane shakes his head. "We were leaving for the arena and that's still what we're going to do."

"I'll be going to the arena with you instead of Josie. Arnold said you can call him if you have questions about the new arrangement."

I've never done anything to her, and she's acting like this is the moment she just conquered her greatest nemesis.

Dane meets my gaze, his mouth set in a tense line. We're beat and we both know it.

"I need to pack my stuff," I say.

Monica gives Dane a fake, sweet smile. "I can stay behind and lock up when she's finished."

He narrows his eyes. "I trust her alone in my house. You, not so much. Go to the arena and I'll meet you there."

She opens her mouth to argue, but Dane cuts her off.

"You're not my fucking boss. I'll meet you at the arena."

Monica widens her eyes and then leaves without another word. Something tells me that tiny victory is the only one I'm getting today.

Dane follows me into the guest room, where most of my stuff is still stored. I pick up Mr. Darcy, who is curled up on the bed, and sit down, putting my cat on my lap.

"Well, this sucks," he says, sitting down beside me.

"She's going to try to get you in bed." Tears well in my eyes. "I don't know why she still has it out for me. She got the promotion."

"Hey." He puts his thumb and forefinger on my chin, turning my face so I'm looking at him. "She can try anything she wants and it won't work. I'm with you."

I'm embarrassed by my inability to stop the tears that spill over. My own aunt, the only family I have left, seems to enjoy hurting me.

"You have to trust me, babe," he says, putting his arm around my shoulders.

"I do. It's not that." I take a deep breath. "I

have to accept that my aunt is never going to like me, don't I?"

"I'd do a hell of a lot more than that if I were you. Tell her to fuck off. You don't need the money from that job. I've got you."

I lean against his shoulder, grateful for his strong, steady presence.

"You may not be able to travel with the team anymore, but I still want you here," he says. "You're not packing anything. My bed is your bed now."

I look up at him. "It's really soon for that."

He shrugs. "Your aunt forced our hand. You're not leaving."

"I'm glad we decided that," I say wryly.

He kisses my forehead. "You know you want to stay. We're good together."

"So you're saying you, me and Monica will all live here together?"

"Yep. And I'll do my best to make you scream my name in bed at two a.m. because fuck her."

I laugh at the mental image. "This is going to get awkward. You know that, right?"

"Awkward for her. Not for us."

"I don't want her seeing you in just your boxers."

He grins. "Jealous?"

"Maybe."

"I'll make sure I'm dressed outside the bedroom."

I cringe. "You'll have to share a hotel room with her when you're traveling."

My heart pounds at the thought of Monica in skimpy pajamas, alone in a hotel room with Dane. I've never been the jealous type, but nothing like this has ever happened to me.

"It'll be okay."

I scoff and meet his gaze. "How would you feel if I was going to be spending multiple nights alone in a hotel room with a single, attractive man?"

"I mean...I'd fucking kill him."

"Exactly."

"But Monica's not attractive."

I glare at him, but his expression remains serious. "She's nowhere close to you, Jo. You're so sexy you make me crazy. You're the only one I want."

Warmth pools in my stomach despite the crummy Monica development. I take his hand and squeeze it, grateful for his reassurance.

"I'm sorry, but I have to go," he says. "Come in the usual entrance for the game tonight, I'll make sure your name's on the list."

"I may find something to wear in your closet."

His lips curve up in a smile. "Good. I'll see you there."

With a final kiss, he leaves. I cuddle with Mr. Darcy for a few more minutes before finally facing reality.

I have to go into the office and talk to my aunt.

twenty-six

JOSIE

It feels different here. When I stepped off the elevator and into the offices of JG Publicity, I used to feel like a true professional. Part of a highly regarded team. A woman who might have been a hot mess on the inside but who could put aside her financial woes and lackluster love life from eight to five every weekday and get shit done.

Now, though, I just see a bunch of coworkers who could do better than this place. There's Tom, who works late often and was only allowed to take one day off when his wife had a baby because Jane said she couldn't risk losing the account he was in charge of.

And Linda, who spends money from her own pocket to cover the difference when my cheap aunt doesn't give her enough cash to pay for the gourmet coffees and lunches she sends Linda to pick up for her.

"Josie," Linda says as she sees me walking in. "It's so good to see you. How are you?" She walks out from behind her desk and gives me a hug. "Gosh, you look great."

I do look great. I wore a new black suit with heels so I'd feel more confident about this meeting.

"Thanks, Linda, you too. I've missed you."

She pulls away and gives me a sympathetic look, glancing over both shoulders before speaking in a low tone. "I'm sorry about the promotion."

I wave a hand, trying to look like I'm over it. I'm not, though. In reality, I have a sick, churning feeling in my stomach.

"It's okay. Is she in?"

Linda knows who I mean—Jane is the universal *she* in this office.

Nodding, Linda leans in and says, "Monica's been asking her for the Mammoths account since you got it. I think she wants to get a hockey player boyfriend out of it."

My stomach churns double time at that. I trust

Dane, but just the thought of Monica trying to charm him makes me stabby. I hate the idea of them alone in a hotel room, even if he was wearing pants and a snow parka because he'd still look sexy as hell.

"Well, she got what she wanted. As usual."

Linda glances back over one shoulder, then the other. "She's in, but there's a staff meeting starting at eleven thirty."

Ah, the old eleven-thirty staff meeting. I don't miss those. Jane doesn't even order in lunch on those days, even though that meeting time forces people to skip lunch.

"Should I ask her if she can see you?" Linda's eyebrows disappear beneath her bangs. "Or maybe you should just attend the meeting."

I smile. "I'm not attending the meeting. And I'm not asking her permission to talk."

"Oh, but--"

"Don't worry, I'll make sure she knows I didn't run it by you."

Poor Linda constantly worries about losing her job. Jane gets pissed when people walk into her office without going through her first to get scheduled. Linda goes from passive to assertive quickly when it comes to that, feeling like it's somehow her fault.

If Jane knew Linda's the one who told me about Monica getting the promotion, I'm sure she'd do something to make Linda's job a little more hellish.

I turn and walk across the open office area, the cubicle dwellers' domain. Though I get a few waves and nods, I get more curious looks. Everyone knows I was in line for the promotion to senior publicist.

No one has to know I'm shaking inside. I look fabulous. All the nice things Dane says about me are playing on repeat in my head. I've got this.

Jane's office has a glass door set inside a glass wall that's open to the entire main office area. I'm sure my coworkers are not so covertly watching as I grab the door handle, open the door and walk inside.

She looks up from her computer at me, peering over the rim of her glasses. "Josie, I'm busy. You'll need to schedule time with Linda."

"This is the only time I'm available."

Yeah, I just said that. Her lips part with surprise.

"What have I done to make you hate me so much?"

I tried so hard to keep my voice level, but my

emotions crept in. I've wanted to ask her that for years but never had the guts.

"The workplace isn't appropriate for crying."

Her tone is a mix of pity and condescension that makes me swallow my anxiety and steel myself.

"I'm not crying. Do I have feelings? Yes, I'm human. And when my own family member repeatedly does hurtful things to me, I feel hurt. Mission accomplished."

"In this office, I am your boss, Josie. Not your aunt. You know--"

"No, that's bullshit. I'm not the one crossing that line; you are. You crossed it a long time ago and I'm just calling you out."

She stands. "You're on very thin ice right now. I suggest you take a day at home to process your disappointment and return to the office tomorrow."

"Tell me why you took me off the Mammoths account."

"I don't owe you an explanation."

My smile is satisfied. "That's what people say when they don't want to be honest. Tell me, boss to employee, why you did it. I was doing a great job."

Her laugh is humorless. "A great job sleeping with the client? That's so unprofessional and you know it. I could have fired you for it. Maybe I should have."

Before Dane, I would have been mortified by this conversation. Ashamed. But I'm a different woman now. I know my worth.

"Yeah, Dane and I developed feelings for each other. It just started. But in no way did it affect my ability to do my job. Everyone in the organization likes me. And you sent Monica in there? She complains constantly. The team doesn't want to be around that on every road trip."

She holds my gaze in silence for a few seconds. "That's your problem—you just want everyone to like you. You're too much like your mother."

"Finally some honesty."

She points at me and raises her voice, her face reddening. "Watch yourself, Josie."

"That's all I've done since the day you hired me." I fight back the lump in my throat. "Since years before that, actually. I admired you when I was growing up. Not that you care. I wanted to be like you. Why do you think I'm here?" I gesture around the office. "You told me when I was in high school that I could own a business one day, like you, and I—"

I look away, unable to continue.

"You're not tough enough for this business."

I scoff. "Monica's not *tough*. She's a bitch. But she kisses your ass and you fall for it every time."

"I hope this hockey player is worth losing your job." Her tone is loaded with smug satisfaction. "You won't be able to manipulate him like your mother manipulated my brother, you know. You're one of a thousand to him. He won't even remember your name at this time next season."

"I quit. And it's not about him; it's about me. I deserve better than this. Every single person out there"--I point at the main office area and glance out there, where I see half a dozen startled expressions of eavesdroppers--"deserves better. Linda shouldn't have to pay for your pastries and eight-dollar coffees when you don't send her with enough money and no one should have to take calls in the evenings when it's not even urgent. And here's an idea—*be nice*. Treat people who work here like people whose personal lives matter. When Andi's mom was sick last year, you made her quit instead of working part-time and you lost a great employee over that."

She sniffs and looks away. "I know it all seems so easy when you aren't the one behind this desk."

"I know it's not easy. But if you want to get

loyalty, you have to give it. I'd rather wait tables full time and be treated with respect than put up with this place."

She points. "There's the door."

"I'm starting my own business."

The words poured out of my mouth before I had time to think about them. I can practically feel Dane beside me, encouraging me to not just walk away but *fight*.

My aunt laughs. She actually *laughs*.

"Good luck with that."

"Thanks. I've already got an investor."

She narrows her eyes. "Which you spread your legs for."

Even with as far as I've come, it hurts. Cruelty from the only family I have left cuts deep, but at least I know now that this is all she's capable of.

You need to do this. You've got a great mind for it. I've got your back.

Dane's encouragement propels me to stand up for myself in a way I never have before.

"You said Dane won't remember my name in a year, but you know what? *You will.* You'll curse my name every time you walk into this office and find out I signed one of your clients or secured another top-tier account. I'll have the best people in the area working for me because they'll know they're part of a team with a boss who values them. You can keep Monica; she's worthless anyway."

My heart is pounding harder than ever before as I turn and open the door to the office, blood rushing in my ears.

Holy. Shit. I just did that.

I keep my chin up as I stride back across the office. My coworker Damian is crouched down in his cubicle, out of sight as he grins and gives me a thumbs-up. Another colleague, Erin, is holding up a piece of paper for me to read with a message written in black marker.

That was fucking AMAZING!!

I smile because it was amazing. I was amazing. And while I'm terrified about whether I can really do this, I'm also excited. Hopeful.

"I'll send someone to pick up my things," I tell Linda.

She nods, not willing to risk being seen talking to me, but the smile she's fighting gives her away.

What will I name my new company? I think about it as I step back onto the elevator. I suppose FJG Publicity lacks subtlety, so I'll have to pass on that one.

It sure has a nice ring to it, though.

twenty-seven

DANE

Not only has Monica taken over the counter of my hotel bathroom with cosmetics and hair products, but she left a cloud of hair spray and stank it up with her perfume.

I just want her to leave me alone, but she talks nonstop. Last night, when I was texting Josie from my bed, Monica chattered about herself the entire time. She's twenty-three, but it feels like I have a teenage girl attached to my hip.

"You know that plan I was telling you I came up with to turn around your image? I got it all written up and we can go over it on our next flight. It has nine actionable steps for you."

I slide on my suit jacket and shake my head. "My image is fine. I'm going to catch the bus."

Since the second I woke up this morning, I've been ready to get on the bus to the Seattle arena where we're playing today. After several days of having Monica around, I look forward to any break I can get from her.

She picks up an obnoxiously large handbag and says, "Okay, I'm ready."

I wasn't waiting for her. Still, she follows me, her tall heels clopping on the tile of the room's entryway.

"Your job is to play hockey. My job is to take care of your image for you. Some of these things aren't that big, but we really need to get some distance between you and the incident with the fan that blew up on social media. I still can't believe Josie let that happen. I mean, she's--"

I give her a pointed look. "How many times do I have to tell you not to mention my girlfriend?"

Monica scoffs. "I'm here because of her incompetence. I can't do my job if I'm not educating you on her mistakes."

I step onto the elevator, my aggravation rising

fast and hard. "I'm not interested in your education. If you have to follow me, fine. But do it silently."

"Dane." She gives me a hurt look just as my teammate Dalton pushes the elevator doors open so he can step on.

"Morning," he says to us.

"Morning," I grumble.

The ride to the main level is silent and awkward, Dalton motioning for Monica to step off first and giving me a look when her back is facing us. I scowl back.

"I need coffee," Monica says brightly. "That coffee in our room was a joke."

I see the bus parked outside and head toward it, walking past her.

"Dane!" she calls after me. "Can't you at least come with me to get coffee?"

"I think you can handle it." My tone is clipped with aggravation.

She closes the distance between us, her heels clacking on the floor once again. This time, she speaks to me in a low tone that only I can hear.

"We're supposed to be a team. We can have disagreements, but we need to do that privately. In public, we need to be a united front."

I huff out a single note of laughter. "I already have a team, and you're not on it."

I stalk off in the direction of the bus. Josie was right. Monica is un-fucking-bearable. It's so obvious what she's trying to do. From her skimpy pajamas to her pouty expressions, I know she wants to get closer to me than Josie is.

There's no chance of that. At least half of my shitty mood is due to being apart from Josie. I miss her, but I'm proud of her for quitting her job and standing up to her aunt.

Thinking of her makes me take out my phone and send her a good morning text. She's been busy the past few days, working on stuff to open her own business.

I feel a stab of irritation when she doesn't respond immediately to my text. She's become my person, and I'm not used to having to wait to talk to her. It's irrational. I didn't want to be tied down until I met her, and now I'm salty over not seeing her for a few days.

As soon as I sit down on the bus, my teammate Aaron flops into the seat next to me.

"Check this out. Amara drew all over herself with markers." He holds up his phone and I see a photo of his young daughter wearing just a diaper, blue, red and purple marker scribbles covering her all over. Even her face has both cheeks and her chin covered.

"Oh, shit." I laugh at the image and Aaron grins, as amused as I am.

"Elena said it took her forty minutes to scrub all of it off."

"Damn. You're gonna owe her a nice date night after this trip."

He looks at the photo of his daughter again, his expression soft. "She's a trip, man."

Monica gets on the bus and scans faces, looking for me. I slump down in my seat, hoping to avoid her.

No such luck. She finds me and heads my way, giving Aaron an apologetic look. "Hey, can I steal that seat from you?"

"Don't move," I tell him in a low tone.

Monica gives me an aggravated look. "Seriously?"

"Seriously."

She huffs out a sigh and walks toward the back of the bus. Aaron looks over at me, a brow arched in amusement. "Guess the new girl's not working out so well?"

"It's fucking ridiculous. I'm going to talk to Coach about it. She ruins my vibe."

Aaron scoffs. "Surely you can figure it out."

I shake my head. "There's bad blood between her and Josie. She got a promotion that should've gone to Josie. For some reason, she hates Josie, and she's trying to get her claws into me."

Aaron lowers his brows, looking serious. "How can anyone hate Josie?"

"Beats me. Might be that Monica's just immature. She's only twenty-three."

My phone buzzes with an incoming text and I take it out of my pocket.

Josie: Good morning! How's it going with the hellbeast?

Dane: Sucks. And I miss you.

Josie: I miss you too.

Dane: You should fly here for the game tonight and stay with me after.

Josie: I wish I could, but I'm going to look at three office spaces today with the realtor and this evening I'm having drinks with a client of mine from JG that I'm trying to get to follow me to my business.

Dane: It's not an attractive male client, is it?

Josie: No one compares to you.

Dane: That's what I like to hear. What about tomorrow? Can you fly to Nashville for my game?

Josie: If I can get a late afternoon flight.

Dane: You've got my credit card to pay for it. I don't care how much it costs, just get there.

Josie: Okay. I can't wait to see you.

Dane. Same here, babe. I'll work on getting Monica a separate room.

Josie: Or not. She can listen to us going at it, I don't care.

Dane: She's a boner killer. I'll get rid of her for the night.

Josie: I have to take a shower. See you tomorrow night. xoxo

Dane: See you soon, gorgeous. Have a good day.

twenty-eight

JOSIE

"Thanks, have a good night," I tell my Uber driver as I rush out of his sedan at the front entrance to the Nashville arena.

Glancing at my watch, I groan when I see the time. Eighteen minutes to puck drop. Dane sent me an electronic ticket to a premium front-row seat right on the glass, where he said Jenn would be waiting for me. When he looks at the seat at game time, I want to be there.

I barely caught my flight here on time. Since deciding to start my own business, I've been on the go every waking minute. It's been worth it, though.

I secured an office space yesterday and I've scored two clients already. I poached both of them from Jane, which feels extra good.

Garver Publicity offers boutique services, which is basically a positive spin on the fact that I'm just getting started and hardly have any clients or employees.

I'm excited about what I do have, though, and about how quickly I've managed to put it together. Both Linda and Erin have put in their two-week notices with Jane so they can come work for me.

It was scary, making this leap and taking the money Dane offered me. But the new and improved Josie believes in herself relentlessly. I went back to my newly leased office space alone yesterday evening, crying as I stood in the recently renovated downtown warehouse space.

My aunt forced me to jump off this cliff, but I've already found my wings. It felt incredible being able to offer Linda and Erin salaries that are twenty percent higher than what Jane pays them. They both deserve it. I told them we're going to build this business together, and it's going to be an inclusive, peaceful, collaborative environment.

"Ticket, ma'am?" an usher asks me when I reach a ticketing gate.

I pass him my phone and he scans the barcode, then points me in the direction I need to go.

As I descend the concrete steps to reach the front row, I take in the view of the rink. The ice is smooth and perfectly polished, ready for skate blades. I've never been so close to a game.

Dane got me this seat so I won't have to see Monica, who's either with Arnold or in the team's friends-and-family section of seats. I'm happy, and seeing her would ruin my good mood.

By the time I reach my seat, I'm sweaty and probably flushed. Jenn stands up from her seat and greets me with a warm smile and a hug.

"Hey, girl," I say. "Thanks for sitting here with me."

"Anytime. I love watching games up close." She eyes me as I exhale heavily. "You okay?"

"Yeah, I've just been moving nonstop for the past twelve hours. I even worked on the flight here. I'm so happy I came, though. I needed this."

The lights go down and the pregame show starts. My gaze is locked on the visiting team's bench, my heart racing with excitement when I see Mammoths players coming out.

There's Dane. He looks over at me and I grin like a teenager with a crush. The day has felt chaotic, but seeing him makes me immediately relax.

The game starts and I force myself to follow the puck instead of Dane. Though I do get to see plenty of him, too, because he and Dalton are passing the puck back and forth.

"Aiden told me about your job thing," Jenn says, leaning over while keeping her eyes on the game. "I'm glad you're going into business for yourself and we're here to support you however we can."

"Thank you, I really appreciate it. I've already found an office space and hired two people."

She glances at me, grinning. "That's amazing!" Returning her gaze to the ice, she slams her hands on the glass as Aiden battles with a Nashville player for the puck. "Fight for it, baby! Don't let him get away!"

She's her husband's biggest fan, and the closer Dane and I get, the more I realize how important it is to me that we have the same kind of relationship.

He believes in me more than anyone ever has. I wish my mom could have met him because he's exactly the kind of man she always hoped I'd choose for myself.

Jenn slumps back against her seat as Nashville

regains control of the puck and all the players head for the other end of the ice.

"Has Dane told you about my brother?" she asks.

"I don't think so."

"He's in real estate. I called him earlier and told him how great you are and he said he'll hire you."

The Mammoths' fans in the crowd cheer as Lucas, the Mammoths' goalie, saves a goal by blocking the puck with his leg.

"That was nice of you, thanks," I say. "I'd love to meet with him sometime. Does he sell residential or commercial real estate?"

She looks confused for a second. "Oh, he doesn't sell real estate. I mean, I guess he does sometimes, but it's not really him selling it. He owns a bunch of real estate. His business name is Hudson Enterprises. You should look him up."

I momentarily forget the game just feet away from us. "Jenn. Is your brother Michael Hudson?"

"I call him Mikey, but yup. You've heard of him?"

For a few seconds, all I can do is laugh. "Heard of him? He's one of the most successful business owners in all of Minneapolis. My aunt has been trying to court him away from his current PR firm for *years*."

She grins. "Well, he's yours now. I'll send you Mikey's number. He's a delegator, just so you know. He likes to hire people and have them work independently."

I side hug her, tears welling in my eyes. "How will I ever thank you for this? Just to get a meeting with him is such an opportunity."

"You're my friend, of course I'll look out for you. You're going to smash it with this business; I know it." She jumps up and I join her, returning my focus to the game. "Get it, Dane!"

Dane comes around the net from behind it and he slides the puck in it from the corner, his teammates surrounding him right after he scores a goal.

As he skates away from the net, he looks at me and puts his gloved hand over his heart. I put my palm over my heart, my chest expanding as I fall a little more in love with him.

"That man would crawl through glass for you." Jenn gives me an impressed look. "I've never seen him like this."

"I'm pretty crazy about him, too," I admit.

For the rest of the game, we laugh and cheer so

loud my throat is sore when the Mammoths win 5–4. We eat hot dogs and nachos and each drink a lukewarm, overpriced beer. I didn't realize how much I was missing time with my best friend, Lina, who is caring for her mom in Texas as she battles cancer.

As Jenn and I wait for the guys to walk out of the locker room after the game, I order Lina some flowers, wine, books and chocolates. I don't want to be one of those women who neglect friendships because she's in a relationship. Lina and I talk on the phone when she can, but it's not often.

I open my schedule and make a note to book myself a flight to visit her and her mom. When I slide my phone into my bag and look up, I lock eyes with Monica.

She's wearing the exact same jersey I am, with Dane's number on it. A familiar flare of worry and annoyance flickers through me as a smug smile plays on her lips.

"She could pass for a high school student," Jenn says from beside me.

At the sound of deep male voices, we turn and see several players dressed in suits walking out of the locker room. One of them is Dane, who locks eyes with me and smiles.

I can't wait for him to get to me, so I meet him halfway, practically flying into his arms.

"I'm so glad you're here," he says in my ear.

"Me too. Great game."

Dane scored two of his team's five goals tonight, including the game-winning one.

"There was this woman I was trying to impress," he says playfully.

I lean back and smile up at him. "Lucky girl."

"I'm not sharing you tonight. If anyone asks us to go out, tell them fuck no."

"I think I'll let you tell them that, actually."

"Dane, I need you for a few minutes," Monica says from nearby.

My excitement at seeing Dane fades as we both turn to look at her.

"I told you I'll be busy with my girlfriend until tomorrow."

She purses her lips in annoyance. "I set up an interview for you. We need to get going."

"I'm leaving with Josie. Cancel the interview and don't set up any more."

He takes my hand and leads me toward the exit, Monica hot on our heels.

"Arnold won't like this. He wants good publicity,

not 'you shall not ass' hashtags and photos of you with your flavor of the week."

Dane stops. I look over at him and say, "Ignore her. She's just trying to get under your skin."

He turns to face Monica, who is glaring at him with a brow raised and a hand on her hip.

"Did you just call Josie my *flavor of the week*?"

She scoffs. "Yeah. It's not like she's wife material. And you were told no women. Dane, you can either come with me, or I'm calling Arnold."

"We're done." His tone is measured, but I also hear a note of fury. "I don't just mean tonight; I mean permanently. When you call Arnold, you let him know he can keep either you or me. Not both. I won't dress for the next game unless you've been fired."

He squeezes my hand as we walk away, my heart racing with a mixture of adoration and trepidation. Dane is risking his career over this.

Once we're out of earshot, I say, "I don't want you losing your place on your team over me. Monica is annoying, but I'm used to it."

"No one talks about you that way and gets away with it. Arnold made his point, and if he thinks this team is better off without me, I'll let him make that call."

"But if you get traded--"

"I won't." He looks around to make sure no one is within earshot. "My teammates are with me on this. I talked to them after the game. Either Monica gets fired or none of us are dressing for the next game. Arnold will fire her. There's not a doubt in my mind."

"Are you sure?" My voice is nearly a whisper.

"About Arnold? Or about us?"

My heart pounds hard as I say, "Both."

He cups my cheek and smiles. "I love you, Nosy. You had me at *'touch my cat and I'll stab you in your sleep.'* And when I'm in, I'm all in. No one mistreats my girl and gets away with it. Got me?"

Love for him swells in my chest. "Got it. And I love you, too."

He leans down to kiss me, and just before his lips reach mine, I murmur, "Obviously you're getting laid tonight."

He laughs. "Obviously."

After a quick, soft kiss, he leads me from the arena to the car waiting for us in the parking lot. Neither of us looks back as the car pulls away. That's where the past is, and we're finally completely focused on our present and future.

epilogue

DANE

SIX WEEKS LATER

"Whoa, Saffron. Let's get a snack later."

The horse I'm riding at Linc and Trinity's Wyoming ranch pays no attention to me, which comes as no surprise. This is the fourth day we've been here and every day, we've gone horseback riding. Every day, Saffron has had a mind of her own.

Today, she's decided to detour from the group and snack on a bush not far from the trail. Nothing I say convinces her to move, so I gently dig my heels into her side the way Linc showed me.

"I'll give you some carrots later, okay? We have to get back to the group."

The pretty gray horse turns her head back in protest but moves anyway. She clops back onto the fresh trail and I see Josie on her horse, Nutmeg.

The group of ten slows down to let me catch up, and soon, Saffron and I are back in earshot.

"Even having a rose shoved up your ass wouldn't improve the smell of your shits," my teammate Justin says.

I wrinkle my brow, realizing I missed a key part of this conversation. But the fact that it includes a rose has to mean they're talking about the *Celebrity Singles* show Dalton is leaving here tomorrow to start filming. We've been chirping at him nonstop about it since he signed the deal to do it.

It's a good idea, but that doesn't mean we won't make fun of him over it for the rest of his life. That's what teammates do. He needs a distraction after we choked in the first round of the playoffs a month ago. Our team hadn't made the playoffs for seven years, and our fans were crazy excited.

All of us felt like we let them down more than anyone else. It sucked having Josie watching us get our asses handed to us at every game. It was especially hard for Dalton, who was in his first season as team captain.

The last mile of our horseback riding is slow. All eight of us who are visiting are still taking in the scenery. It's like a painting. There are tall mountains in the distance, vibrant green trees, fields of tall grass and colorful wildflowers. And the sunsets here are spectacular.

Linc came to watch us in the playoffs, and when he offered a stay at his ranch to anyone who wanted a getaway to shake it off, several of us took him up on it. In addition to me, Josie, Jenn, Aiden, Dalton, Justin, Tate and our trainer, Gina, are all here.

Josie has become great friends with Jenn, Elena and Gina, and she's getting closer to Trinity on this trip. Not only does she fit into our group perfectly, but I fit in better than I ever have now that I've settled down with her.

As soon as we get back to the newly built stables, Josie's horse takes a massive shit. She grabs the shovel Linc showed us how to shovel horse shit with, but I take it from her.

She gives me an amused look. "You think I'm too precious to shovel shit?"

"He just loves horseshit," Aiden quips. "Almost as much as he loves bullshit. You'll see."

I flip him off with my free hand before cleaning up the mess. The women all want to brush the horses, so we do that before heading for the screened-in porch for an afternoon drink.

Linc and Trin did an incredible job on the renovation of this place. They had the main lodge completely updated and they added on to and remodeled the guesthouse. There are new heated and air-conditioned quarters for their eleven rescued dogs. They also have several cats, four goats, eleven horses and a bunch of chickens.

The massive screened-in porch was a new addition, as was an in-ground pool and hot tub.

Tate slides behind the bar on the porch and starts serving drinks, starting with glasses of wine and amaretto stone sours for the women.

"Do I smell like a horse?" Jenn asks Josie.

Josie sniffs her. "Yep. But I think we all do."

"We'll get in the pool later," Aiden says. "That'll take care of it."

Jenn shakes her head. "There's no soap in the pool. You have to take a shower before bed tonight."

He gives her a ridiculous smolder. "You know you love my man musk, baby. It's my pheromones that make you jump me every night."

She laughs as Tate passes her a glass of wine. "Yeah, no. I spend enough time smelling your sweaty hockey gear. You can at least shower on vacation."

Josie slides onto my lap, a bottle of water in hand. "Don't forget we're making dinner tonight."

I groan because cooking sucks. We divided it up, though, because none of us wants Linc and Trin cooking for us every night.

"What are we making?"

"Steak and shrimp fajitas."

"I'll try not to drink so much beer that I fall onto the grill."

She shrugs. "I'd still do you if you had grill marks on your face."

"That's true love," Gina says from nearby.

Dalton hands Dane a fresh beer, then gets everyone's attention. He raises his bottle into the air.

"I'd like to propose a toast to myself in honor of my upcoming appearance on *Celebrity Singles*. I expect you all to have watch parties every week when it's done filming and spend every minute of every day on social media making sure I'm trending."

"You're gonna be the first one voted off the island," Tate says.

"There's no island. And Archer found his true love on a reality show, remember?"

"Who else is going to be on this show?" Lincoln asks.

"No idea. None of us are allowed to know until we get there." Dalton glares at him. "Anyway, back to my toast."

"Are you even looking for love, though?" Trinity asks her brother. "Last time you were here you said you like being single."

Dalton lowers his bottle, looking agitated. "I'm...looking for exposure."

"Bro. Do not expose yourself. It's not a good way to pick up women," Justin says.

"Especially not when your dick's as small as his," Tate adds.

Dalton sighs heavily. "Will you fuckers stop? I proposed a toast."

"No one proposes a toast to themselves," Linc says. "That's where you went wrong."

"Fine." Dalton raises his bottle again. "A toast to all the women I'm going to meet."

"Such a bad idea," I say to Josie. "Seriously, what's your professional opinion?"

She cringes, looking apologetic. "I mean...there are some scenarios where it could be good."

"But more where it could be bad."

"Yeah? Those shows with marriage proposals at the end are always pretty...soapy, I guess. They don't seem real. Everyone's sleeping with everyone. At least it seems like it."

Dalton shakes his head and tips back his beer, abandoning his toast.

"I think we should go shower," I say. "I'm sweaty from being outside so much."

The corners of Josie's lips tilt up slightly in a smile because she knows I really want sex followed by a shower. Her business is booming, which is great, but we've never had this much time together with neither of us working. We've been making the most of it.

"A shower would be good."

Aiden grins at Jenn. "Maybe we should *take a shower*, too, babe."

She laughs. "Oh, now he's willing to wash off the horse smell."

"After six years of marriage, I'd wash off my own skin for a blow job," he mutters.

"I'll remember that later."

He makes a heart shape with his hands. She shakes her head but can't keep from smiling.

I stand up, surprising Josie by scooping her into my arms as I do.

"I guess we're going right now," she says.

"Damn right." I look around at the faces in the room, smirking. "Don't wait up, kids."

"You're making dinner," Tate calls as we leave the room. "We want to eat before midnight!"

Josie wraps an arm around my neck, still holding her glass of wine.

"Are you having fun?" I ask her.

"Are you kidding? I'm having an amazing time. How about you?"

I kiss her. "I'm with you. That's all I need."

"God, I love you."

"Love you too, babe."

I carry her upstairs then, relishing every minute of our first vacation together. It's one of many firsts, and I can't wait to experience all of them with the woman of my dreams.

Thank you for reading Drawn to You! If you enjoyed it, I would really appreciate a review wherever you bought it.

If you want more from the Mammoths NOW, my standalone book Exiled is the story of Archer and Lauren. Check it out HERE.

The next book in the Mammoths series is Changed by You.

also by brenda rothert

CHICAGO BLAZE SERIES

Book 1 - Anton

Book 2 - Luca

Book 3 - Victor

Book 4 - Knox

Book 5 - Alexei

Book 6 - Easy

Book 7 - Jonah

Book 8 - Kit

Book 9 - Olivier

COLORADO COYOTES SERIES

Book 1 - The Donor

Book 2 - The Opponent

Book 3 - The Proposal

Book 4 - The Imposter

Book 5 - The Face-Off

SIN CITY SAINTS SERIES

Book 1 - Maverick

Book 3 - Drawn Deeper

Book 4 - Hidden Depth

Filthy Series

Book 1 - Dirty Work

Book 2 - Dirty Secret

Book 3 - Dirty Defiance

Standalones

Come Closer

Buried

Sweet Sixteen

His

Alpha Mail

Healing Touch

Barely Breathing

Exiled

Unspoken

Brenda Rothert lives in Central Illinois with her husband, children and three dogs. She loves to hear from readers through her website or her Facebook Group, Rothert's Readers.

www.ingramcontent.com/pod-product-compliance
Lightning Source LLC
Chambersburg PA
CBHW011320310726
48973CB00011B/2995